OLIVER GRUFFLE

SECRETS OF HARMONY HAVEN

Book 1

The Runaways

OLIVER GRUFFLE

SECRETS OF HARMONY HAVEN

Book 1

The Runaways

Anna Southwell

PARTNER PUBLISHING

BEACHY BOOKS

First published by

Beachy Books Partner Publishing in 2020

(an imprint of Beachy Books Limited)

www.beachybooks.com

1

A CIP catalogue record for this book is available from the British Library.

ISBN: 978-1-913894-00-9

Set in Atten Round New

With my love I dedicate this book

to my family –

For all my grandchildren 'who wanted a story'

written with love – Nanny Quakers.

In loving memory of Kim, a treasured Border collie,

who was such a joy to my family.

And to all who love the beauty of the Isle of Wight –

truly, a magical Island!

Anna Southwell

INSPIRATION FOR OLIVER GRUFFLE

Having a lifetime of love for the Isle of Wight and a love of all animals was my inspiration for this story.

My love of animals began when, as a child on the Island, I came across a large colony of coloured feral kittens. Not having a pet of my own, I decided that I would rescue one or two. I spent three hours in 'cat heaven' because I was so desperate to have a pet of my own. It was a sad and hard lesson to learn that those feral cats did not want me to rescue them and they remained wild. But, the happy memories have stayed with me.

My life has been enriched by the many different animals I have cared for, all so different in character, which I show in this story. As an Island vet once said to me, 'We should never forget that, just like us, animals have feelings too!'

My last cat was from a rescue home and was dearly loved. She was a FERAL cat!

Anna Southwell

ACKNOWLEDGEMENTS

The author would like to thank Philip Bell, publisher at Beachy Books, for his help and guidance in publishing the book, and to illustrator, Joanna Scott, for the wonderful and colourful visualisation of Oliver Gruffle that so captured his personality and kindness, and the charming end-page illustration. Thank you both!

CONTENTS

CHAPTER 1

FOOD HEAVEN

Pickle felt miserable, in fact, he wondered if any other pig on the Isle of Wight, where he lived, could ever feel as miserable as he was feeling today.

With saddened eyes he watched his companions snorting and honking, as they searched the muddy field for something to eat. Their feet squelching, as they trod in the thick mud that was all around them. Pickle was hungry too; there was never enough food put in the trough for so many pigs, and his tummy rumbled constantly from hunger.

The man who owned the farm was called Farmer Muggleton and Pickle knew this man had no love for the animals he kept in his care. Along with many of the other pigs, Pickle had red weals of raised skin across his back, from constantly being lashed with a cane. And this was just one of the reasons why the farmer was disliked and feared by all the animals on the farm.

Although Pickle felt very sad today, his life knew some happiness as he was lucky to have two very dear friends. His oldest friend was a dog, a black and white

Border collie. Pickle called him Pal, because that was just what he was—a loving friend. And Pickle loved him dearly.

Most days Pal would chat to his friend through the hedgerow, and the little pig loved to listen to his friend's wise words. He would tell him stories about the Isle of Wight—exciting stories about the beautiful countryside, the sandy beaches and the sea.

Pal also told him about dinosaurs and other kinds of prehistoric creatures that roamed the Island long ago. And if Pickle could not imagine what a beach or anything else was like, Pal would describe it to him.

But as he chatted, Pal would keep a constant lookout, just in case Farmer Muggleton would creep up behind him, because he too was afraid of this fearsome man. Pal would tell his friend that people who bullied others were usually cowards themselves and would 'freak-out' if it was them being bullied!

Pickle's other close friend was called Patsy. She was the most beautiful pink pig he had ever seen in his life, and he adored her, especially her little curly tail, which he would give a gentle pull on with his mouth to surprise her! The truth was Pickle and Patsy were in love.

How he wished he could give her a happier life to

what they had now; a happier life like the one he had known before he came to this farm. His mind then started to drift back in time to those early memories, so much so, tears began to fall from his eyes and trickled down his cheeks. How sweet his memories were of life before with the kind and gentle people that had looked after him since he was born. He never forgot their names—Mr and Mrs Onion. They didn't have a farm because they only kept a few animals as a hobby. It was called a smallholding, which is much smaller than a farm.

He remembered there were goats who gave plenty of milk, from which Mr and Mrs Onion were able to make cheese and yoghurt, and then sold to the local people. There were dogs and quite a few cats and kittens, and lots of chickens and ducks. And of course, a lovely pink cuddly pig called Blossom. She was Pickle's Mum.

Mr and Mrs Onion had no children, but they loved all their animals—which they thought of as their own children. All the animals were well cared for, had plenty to eat and always had a good supply of clean bedding in their pens, situated in a large barn. They never wanted for anything.

In fact, their local vet, who was a very nice, kind man called Mr Sam, said all the animals in their care were spoilt, and that, with all the kind attention they received, he wouldn't mind being an animal there himself!

How happy the owners were when Blossom the pig had her little family. And it was a small family compared to the twelve or more piglets that some pigs have. Blossom had four piglets—two girls that were called Relish and Spring, and two boys, Gherkin and Pickle.

Mr Sam would always tickle Pickle's tummy and called him the best Pickle Onion he had ever seen. So, Pickle liked his name very much, because it made people laugh and when they were laughing, he knew they were happy. But then came the sad times, the day his loving owners stayed in their home and never came out to feed or check on their animals. It was something that had never happened before.

So, something very serious had happened but none of the animals knew what...

Later that day there was a lot of activity and noise in the yard. Jeeps with trailers, horse boxes and vans began arriving. The commotion made all the animals aware something terrible was about to happen.

Strange people were walking everywhere and inspecting the animals. Pickle clearly remembered squealing loudly as he was rough-handled, and his brother and sisters did the same.

Pickle remembered shivering with fright and cuddling into his mother to feel safe when a large group of people surrounded their pen. One man began shouting loudly, whilst others waved their hands about and nodded their heads back to him. Pickle found out later that he was in an auction where all the animals were being sold to the highest bidder.

He also learnt that day, never to take anything for granted, because gone was all the tasty food and treats, the love and the comfort of a happy home. Gone was his cuddly Mummy, his brother Garnish and his two sisters, Relish and Spring, as well as all his friends. Because that same day he became the property of the man who had rough-handled him—Farmer Muggleton!

Pickle then stopped daydreaming about the past. He shook his head in despair as he looked around at the dozens of other pigs in the muddy field. He noted the run-down pigsties, so draughty, which always had the lowest quantity of straw on the ground inside them. He felt so sad as he looked around. His life was so very different now. How he wished he could change it for the better again! But at least he had his memories of his happy past to comfort him.

Hunger made Pickle move towards the food troughs, knowing they would be empty by now. But he, still looked anyway, hoping to find a morsel. He then searched amongst the mud, hoping to find a potato skin, or some bread crusts, but there was nothing there either.

As he lifted his head from the ground, he suddenly spotted Pal, his dog friend, looking through the farm gate and trying to attract his attention. Pickle knew a quick chat with his dear friend would make him feel happier, so he trotted over to meet him.

'Hello Pal, how are you today?' he asked, trying his best to sound cheerful.

'Never mind how I am, Pickle—just listen to me!' he barked. 'I have something very important to say to you. And I must be quick before Farmer Muggleton misses me!'

'I'm listening—what's the matter?' Pickle couldn't help but notice his friend had a very worried look on his face.

'I'm leaving, Pickle,' Pal said. 'I'm running away from this horrible farm and I want you and Patsy to come with me.'

'Run away, Pal!' squealed Pickle. 'I've never run away

before! I think I would be very scared of the dangers around, and I'd not even know where to run too! What made, you suddenly decide to do this?' The little pig was aware his snout was twitching nervously. 'And if you go on your own, I might never see you again—I'd be losing my best friend!'

Pal looked sadly at the little pig; he hated to tell him what he knew. But Pickle was his dear friend and he had no choice. Pal poked his muzzle through the gate to be nearer to the piglet, as he told him, as kindly as he could, that there was a serious danger ahead for him if he stayed on this farm.

'You have to come with me—you must leave to-morrow!' insisted Pal. 'Take a look at that lorry in the farmyard. Do you see the writing on the side of it says, "Muggleton's Sausages"! And what does he use to make those?!— yeah!—it's PIGS!'

Pal fell silent as he watched his friend twitch even more after what he had just told him. He also noticed the little pig was beginning to tremble. 'I'm sorry Pickle, but sometimes we have to say things that might be hurtful to our friends to protect them. But what I have told you is the truth and you know I always try to talk wisely to you!'

'You mean—you mean—it's my turn and Patsy's to disappear, just like the other pigs before? We are to go to Food Heaven!' Pickle moaned loudly, before he said, in a distressed voice, 'I don't want to die Pal, and I don't want to lose Patsy either. Nor do I want to be made into a sausage!'

'Then you have no choice—you both must come with me!' pleaded the dog sincerely. 'And, I'm sorry to have to tell you this, but I overheard Farmer Muggleton making his plans, and it's all going to happen tomorrow morning, very early. Lots of pigs are going to Food Heaven!' Pal could feel his own eyes filling up with tears as he watched his dear friend trying to take in everything that was being said to him. 'Listen, Pickle! Listen carefully to what I tell you. I've been told this by Scrumpy. Do you remember me telling you about my new friend and how I was kind to him recently? Well, he told me of a secret place, here on the Island where we could live together and be safe and happy for the rest of our lives. It's called "Harmony Haven". You've heard about it too—remember!—but Pickle, the exciting part is, it's not a fairy tale place like we thought it was. It really does exist!'

'And this is where we all would run too?' said Pickle, his eyes bulging.

'Yes Pickle!—this is my plan!' panted Pal.

'But what about all the other pigs here?' interrupted Pickle. 'Can they all come too?'

Pal looked at his friend as he sadly shook his head. 'No, I'm sorry. This must remain our secret only. Because all the trotters would leave a trail in the direction we had walked in, and in no time we would be recaptured. Can you imagine how we would be treated then—for daring to escape!' Pal wiped away a tear from each eye with his paw, as he said quietly to his friend, 'I couldn't bear to lose you Pickle, my best friend, when I know you could be saved if you come with me.'

Usually Pickle loved to listen to everything Pal told him, but today his words were a great shock and the news made him feel quite sick inside. He didn't want to go to Food Heaven and come back as a sausage! He just wanted to marry Patsy and have a family of piglets and live a happy life. But, it was obvious Farmer Muggleton had other plans for them, so he felt he had only one choice—to run away with Pal!

'I'll come Pal,' he whispered back nervously, wondering what the plan would be for their escape. 'And I am sure Patsy will want to do the same.'

Pal was delighted and he lost no time in telling Pickle

exactly what he and Patsy must do. 'You must follow my instructions Pickle, just as I tell you—we are going to only get this one chance to escape. And there can be no mistakes, do you understand?'

Pickle nodded his head and listened carefully to Pal's every word. He remembered every detail of the plan to escape from this terrible farm. When he had finished talking, Pal then added quickly, 'I must rush away now, because I have two very important letters to post for Scrumpy, which I will tell you about tomorrow.' And as an afterthought he stressed, 'Please make sure you both get a good night's sleep and I beg you not to be late meeting me in the morning. And don't forget to keep out of sight at feed time, no matter how hungry you both are!'

Pickle watched as Pal cleverly picked up the two letters off the ground with his mouth. And then he dashed off as fast as he could go, in the direction of the post box. 'Thanks, Pal, for being the best friend anyone could want,' shouted Pickle after him—at the same time he wondered why Pal was posting letters, but then he knew the Border collie dog was a very wise dog indeed and he would find out in time.

CHAPTER 2

THE SECRET PLAN

Pickle now had to find Patsy and tell her the secret. He hoped, with all his heart, that she would want to come with them. He hated the thought of having to tell her what would happen to them if she refused!

After looking for some time, he found her. She was chatting away to her girlfriends. They were discussing girlie-problems and they didn't want Pickle hearing what they were saying, so they all tried to shoo him away.

But today he was having none of that. 'Patsy! Patsy!' he insisted. 'You must come with me, immediately; I need to talk to you about an important matter that just won't wait!' He felt embarrassed as all the girl pigs stared at him. They grunted and giggled, teasing him and Patsy.

'Isn't love grand!' and 'I love you Patsy!' they snorted in a voice that mimicked Pickle's.

Patsy grinned widely as she left her friends, her face now a bright pink glow. But the two of them really didn't mind being teased by their friends, as they all needed some laughter in their lives, on this unhappy farm.

'I'm coming, my darling, Pickle,' she replied cheekily, much to the delight of the girl pigs who, in unison, immediately burst into squeals of laughter.

Pickle then led her well out of earshot of all the other pigs, so they could not hear what he had to say to his girlfriend. And then, as kindly as he could, he told her about the wise talk with Pal. He then added, gently, 'You know Pal is wise. Any dog that can make sheep do as he tells them, and can order ducks into pens as well, has to be wise and very clever. We can trust Pal's every word to be true, believe me! He then watched her face to await the answer he wanted to hear. And he could see that what he had just told her had come as a great shock.

Patsy became very tearful. And she sobbed even louder when she was told that it could only be the three of them that escaped in the morning, and that she was forbidden to tell any of the other pigs about their secret plan.

He nuzzled closer to comfort her. He hated to see her cry. 'Come on my little piggy-wiggy,' he said, affectionately, hoping to raise a smile. 'Please... don't cry. This is our chance to be happy and safe for the rest of our lives. Unless, of course, you fancy being a sausage in Food Heaven!'

Immediately he made his last remark, he wished he hadn't, as she started to cry again, but this time, even louder. 'Ssh, Patsy—ssh! The other pigs are looking at us. I'm sorry. I shouldn't have said that—but just tell me you want to spend the rest of your life with me...'

Patsy returned his nuzzling and stopped crying. And then, to Pickle's delight, she nodded her head in agreement.

Immediately, Pickle started to explain to her what Pal's plan was for their escape. He pleaded with her to follow his instructions carefully, as they were only going to have one chance in the morning to run away.

Wide-eyed, Patsy looked at him and said, dramatically, 'My Mother told me I should always face any problems and not run away from them.'

In reply, Pickle would have liked to have said, 'Well that's why your mother became a sausage!', but he managed to keep his mouth shut and avoided upsetting her again. Then after an awkward pause he continued: 'Patsy, please just do as I say—this is important! You must make sure you get an early night's sleep.' He looked at her guiltily as he added, 'And don't forget to go to the very back of the pigsty to sleep. And please DO NOT come out at feed time, no matter how hungry you are!'

Patsy grunted a nod and then trotted clumsily over the mud to return to her friends. Pickle just hoped she would follow the carefully laid plans and not gossip to her friends by mistake. He knew what she could be like!

The rest of the day seemed to drag by because Pickle was dwelling on the big plan tomorrow. Many a time, he had heard whispers about Harmony Haven, and how it was a safe place for animals and other beings. But he had always thought it was just a legend, but now Pal had confirmed that it was true he couldn't quite believe it—would they really find Harmony Haven?

Every now and then he would give a shiver as he thought about their secret plan. It was a mixture of fear and excitement. But he knew he must be a strong, bold pig for Patsy's sake. Tomorrow just couldn't come fast enough.

Later he met up with Patsy and they decided to relax together in a muddy watery pool. They always enjoyed having a wallow, especially when they had it to themselves.

Eventually, darkness fell, and the pair separated early to go to their own pigsties. They both felt guilty as they pushed their way through the drift of other pigs to jostle for a space at the back, where every pig knew was the warmest place to sleep. The front of the sty was always draughty, with the barest of straw to keep a pig warm.

Pickle began to act out the start of the plan to ensure a place at the back of the pigsty. He pretended to shiver, acted as though he was ill. And soon it was noticed by an older pig called Porker. 'Have you caught a chill, Pickle?' he asked in a concerned voice.

Pickle nodded his head in reply and hoped he wasn't overdoing his shivering act.

'Let Pickle through to the back everyone,' pleaded Porker. 'He's not well at all.'

Immediately there was a lot of activity in the pigsty, as some of the pigs made way for him, whilst others decided to go and sleep elsewhere.

'Don't you sneeze on me Pickle,' said a nearby pig.

Pickle smiled weakly back, and then used some of the straw to cover himself over. He hated to deceive them and, knowing what their fate was going to be to-morrow, it made him feel guilty and very sad.

'I don't think I shall be wanting my food tomorrow. I don't feel well at all,' said Pickle, in a sorrowful voice. 'Maybe you all would like to have my share and thank you for being so kind to me.'

'Well, that's a very kind offer Pickle,' said Porker, beaming. 'And feeling as hungry as I do, I won't refuse it. Now, you get off to sleep and I think you're being wise not to get up in the morning.'

Pickle hid a smile. *Greedy pig!* he thought to himself. He had wanted his food to be shared by them all, but it was obvious Porker had other ideas.

He then snuggled deeper into the straw, but he couldn't sleep. He was glad that his first part of the plan had worked out well. And he was glad that he had shown kindness too, over his food, as it could very well be the last breakfast his companions would ever eat.

Dawn began to break, and Pickle could hear the birds in the nearby trees beginning their dawn chorus of song. Morning light entered the sty through cracks in the old wooden walls. Slowly, all the pigs began to leave the sties and make their way into the field, as ever, all hoping to be first at the troughs, hoping to gobble down the best food.

Pickle now was on his own and, through the cracks, he could see exactly what was happening outside. He could feel tears welling up in his eyes and he wished it could have been possible to have saved all of his companions. He looked around the yard and felt relieved as there was no sign of Patsy.

But then he heard a loud noise—he knew what it was—and as he looked over towards the farm gate, Farmer Muggleton's lorry arrived. Now the bad times were about to start. Through the crack in the wall, he watched as the lorry's ramp, leading inside, was lowered with a clank.

Pickle gulped. He tried to hold his breath for as long as he could, because he was afraid that even breathing too loudly would give him away if the farmer looked inside his pigsty.

'Don't feed them much, son!' he heard Farmer Muggleton tell his helper. 'They won't need food where they're going, but it will keep them quieter in the lorry. Nothing I hate more first thing in the morning is a load of squealing pigs!'

Farmer Muggleton's cane came down over the back

of some of the pigs. They grunted and ran off in despair. Pickle wanted to rush out like a pig gone berserk and bite the pair of horrible men in retaliation or knock them both into the muddy hole! But he knew he must resist that urge, so all he could do was watch in horror.

Then the two farmers swung into action as they began dragging squealing pigs towards the lorry. Time and time again, they repeated the process until they had a lorry full of pigs who were unaware what their fate was going to be.

Pickle watched as the ramp was securely fastened and the field gate secured once more. He gave a sigh of relief; it had been such a sad sight to witness though, and Pickle felt horrible inside. The lorry engine then started up and it slowly drove off. All had happened just as Pal had said. The horror was over.

'Goodbye my friends!' he cried out. But inside he was feeling guilty.

But there was no time now for thought or sadness; he had to follow the next part of Pal's plan immediately. He rushed out of the pigsty and, to his delight, saw Patsy trotting towards him. She was in tears, as most of her girlfriends had been taken.

'Don't tell me, Patsy. I saw it all and it was horrible. But at least we have been spared.' He gave her a gentle nuzzle with his snout. 'Now come on my little piggy-wiggy, let's go as quick as we can, away from this horrible place. There is no time to spare!'

Then together in silence they started to trot as fast as they could go through the thick mud. Pal had direct-ed them to go to the bottom of the field where, in a corner, he knew there was a small gap in the hedge.

Suddenly they saw Pal the other side of the hedge-row and they both felt relieved to see him there.

'I am so glad to see you both,' Pal blurted out in a breathless manner. As he too had to run as fast as he could, as soon as he was sure the lorry was out of sight.

He then started to pull and tug on branches and prickles with his mouth and paws, holding them back to enlarge the gap, so that Pickle and Patsy could scramble through safely, and to each in turn, he urged them to be quick! And when they were safely through, he shouted wildly, 'Run my beauties—run! Come on, follow me!'

The two little pigs didn't have to be told twice, trot-ting quickly after their friend. After some time, he led them into dense woodland, across the road from the field.

'We're free! We're free!' yelled Pal, much to the delight of the two pigs who had never ran so fast in all their lives—but then, they had never run away before.

CHAPTER 3

THE WOODLAND WARDEN

The three friends kept running until they had to stop for breath. But this time, they didn't mind the scratches from the branches that they were getting on their backs, as their minds could only think about getting as far away as possible from the farm.

Pickle and Patsy were trying to catch their breath, unlike Pal, who could have gone on running for ages being a dog, but he stopped to let them catch their breath. 'I think this day is going to be the best one we have had for a long, long time,' Pal said , panting. He gazed at his two friends. 'We cannot rest yet, but we will soon. Remember, this is our first day of freedom and it's going to lead us to happiness. Try and put the bad times behind you.'

'I'm sorry, Pal, if we both look glum, we feel sad for our friends and what could be happening to them at this very moment!' gasped Pickle, in a worried voice. 'I suppose we feel guilty because you are right Pal, we are going to have a good life, but our friends will not be part of it.'

Pal spoke tenderly in reply, 'I understand how you both feel, but we have to forget our unhappy past because we cannot change it.' He then added wisely, 'So, let us all look to the future, which we can change, and which begins—right now!'

Pal watched as the pigs nodded their heads in agreement at what he had just said. 'Are you ready for some more running, because we are not safe yet!' He couldn't help but notice the look of a smile on their faces, which he hoped would get bigger as they got further away from the farm and its unhappy memories.

Pal then took the lead once more as he led his two friends deeper and deeper into the dark woods. Every now and then he would stop to give them a little rest, as they were finding it hard to keep up with him. Pal had his thick coat to protect his skin from scratches, whereas the pigs only had a light coating of hair on their body. But, apart from a cry of 'Ouch!' here and there, they never complained. He knew it was all part of their journey towards a happier life in Harmony Haven.

It was now well into the morning, and the friends seemed to have been running for hours when finally they came across an opening in the woods. There were paths leading to the right and to the left, and well-trodden by looking at the track marks others had left behind.

'Are we lost, Pal?' whispered Patsy, nervously, as she glanced around to see if anyone was about, or if they had been followed.

'Which way do we go now, Pal?' said Pickle in a whisper. He was eager to get away from the clearing and felt much safer in the shelter of the trees and undergrowth, even if they were getting scratched.

'Hush, you two! We are not lost! I know exactly where we have to go. Come on, follow me, quickly!' Pal then darted straight ahead into the dense woodland once again, ignoring the paths on either side, as he had been instructed to do by Scrumpy. But this undergrowth was far thicker than before, and all they could do now was walk and push their way through.

After a while, Pal stopped once again and said happily, 'Scrumpy told me we must now look out for a very old oak tree, which has a massive trunk. I know we are all tired, but we must find it, as it is an important part of our journey.' He gave a laugh as he spoke again. 'Can you imagine it, my friends... we are soon going to be safe!' The sheepdog felt happier, now that they were well away from the farm and he was pleased to see the two piglets looked happier as well.

They scrambled along for a little while longer with a renewed enthusiasm, having Pal's words in their minds, their eyes flashing right and left as they searched for the old oak tree. Soon they came to a small clearing in the wood, and in front of them stood, majestically, the largest oak tree they had ever seen. It's trunk was thick and twisted, and the tree had to be very, very old.

'There it is—look! We've found the oak tree,' gasped Pal, in an excited voice. Whilst Pickle and Patsy were trying their hardest to jump in the air, feeling thrilled and happy that soon they would all be safe.

High above them, in the tree, they could see red squirrels darting amongst the branches. They watched their antics of those running along the woodland floor, gathering acorns to store for winter. They all laughed as they watched the squirrels chasing each other and playing, and when they realised they were actually laughing, they laughed even louder. But then, knowing this was the start of a new life for each of them, they huddled together as friends, and gently sobbed. They cried, not just for their sorrow they had each been through, but for the joy and relief they were each feeling that happiness was not so far away.

The three friends then all gazed at the huge old oak tree that had to be hundreds of years old, judging by the size of the trunk.

'What's the importance of this tree, Pal?' asked Pickle, curiously.

Pal grinned as he spoke excitedly. 'We are meeting someone here who is going to help us get to Harmony Haven. He's called the Woodland Warden, but he won't acknowledge us until I give him a secret sign. So, stand back my friends and give me room, as I have to do exactly as my friend Scrumpy instructed me to do!'

Patsy and Pickle did as he requested, eager to see what the secret sign was that Pal had to give. They watched in amazement and stifled laughter as they watched him twirl three times to the right, and then twice to the left, and then walk on his hind legs around in a circle. After which, he fell to the ground and lay there looking quite dazed, but pleased with himself for completing the secret sign.

'Are you dizzy, Pal?' laughed the two pigs. They could contain their laughter no more. Especially as they watched Pal's eyes rolling.

He didn't get a chance to reply, as all around them was scurrying and chattering in the old oak tree, and also from the surrounding trees. There appeared to be dozens of little red squirrels everywhere. It was as if messages were being sent amongst the red squirrel population. The three friends just stood watching and listening and wondering what would happen next. And then, suddenly, the wood fell silent.

'I believe you are looking for me!' came a squeaky voice from high above the three friends.

They all looked up, but only noticed the leaves on the branches of the oak tree shivering in the breeze.

'Are you the Woodland Warden?' asked Pal, politely, as he strained his head trying to find who had spoken to them.

'I am!' squeaked a reply. 'May I ask your names and what you want of me?'

'My name is Pal and I am a Border collie dog, and my two dear friends here are piglets; this is Patsy and this is Pickle. And we wish to go to Harmony Haven, Sir. We understand we can find happiness there and be safe for the rest of our lives.' Pal called him 'Sir', because he knew this was very respectful way to address an important person.

The voice then asked another question. 'Who told you about Harmony Haven?'

Eagerly, Pal replied, 'It was my friend Scrumpy; he told me that there actually was a place called Harmony Haven and it wasn't just a fairy-tale story that had been passed down through the generations of animals.'

Pickle grunted and butted in, 'Woodland Warden, my friends and I have run away from a very unkind and brutal farmer and we need help desperately, before we are found and sent back there!'

'And Pickle and I were due to go to Food Heaven today and be made into sausages!' added Patsy, anxiously. 'Please, will you help us find this place?'

They still couldn't see who was speaking to them because the voice was hidden behind the branches and leaves. They strained their necks to look amongst the branches of the oak tree, still decorated in bright green leaves, which seemed odd to them as it was autumn and most of the other trees had shed leaves of red and brown onto the ground.

The voice spoke again. 'I see our mutual friend Scrumpy is still playing jokes. I guess it was him that told Pal to spin round in that way?' The voice laughed in a chirpy chuckle. 'All you had to do was call for me, but it was funny watching you doing that dance, so much so, I nearly fell out of the tree!'

Pal laughed quietly to himself; he knew Scrumpy liked to play jokes! But he didn't mind acting foolish in front of his friends as they needed a laugh to cheer them up.

'Can you help us, please?' pleaded Pal, hopefully.

'I can!' came back the instant reply. 'I certainly can, if you can give me the answer to my question... Who is the Guardian of Harmony Haven?'

'It's Oliver Gruffle! It's Oliver Gruffle!' shouted back the three friends in unison, delighted that they all knew the legendary name they had heard stories about for so long.

'Good, you are correct and it is my pleasure to tell you that you all will be going to Harmony Haven!' came the reply, 'If you could only just stop jumping up and down for a minute! It will be me that guides you on the next stage of your journey.'

'Do you hear that Pickle and Patsy?' yelled Pal. 'We've made it!' And with those words he joined in with the jumping up and down, twirling round and round, not caring how dizzy he felt after. They all felt as if they had been walking on hot coals, which was what their paws and trotters felt like after so much walking. Soon they would be safe, they all thought.

'We are forgetting our manners,' said Pal, suddenly. 'We must say thank you to the Woodland Warden for his kind help.'

The three of them gazed upwards, as they now stood still. 'Thank you, Sir. Thank you Warden. But we still can't see you!'

In the quietness that was all around them, now came a rustle in the branches of the oak tree.

'There's someone there!' exclaimed Pickle.

The three friends all took a step backwards, staring in amazement at the strangest of beings looking down at them from above. The little man was very small and very skinny, with knobbly knees and elbows. He was clad in an outfit that looked like the bark of a tree. His hands and face were the same colour as an early acorn—bright green! And on his head he wore a helmet just like the cup of an acorn. He truly looked like a wooden man, complete with a nose that looked like a small doorknob.

But as the friends looked at him, he gave a smile and they could see he had a friendly face. His smile widened and his round large eyes filled with a look of kindness. This was not a being to be feared. He was just very different from themselves.

'Seek and you shall find—hello there!' he said. 'I'm the Woodland Warden, at your service. I'm happy to meet you all and to be of assistance on your journey to Harmony Haven.'

'We have never seen anyone that looks like you!' said Pal, dramatically and not meaning to offend. 'May I respectfully ask... are you an animal?'

The Woodland Warden laughed. 'I'm what is known as a "galoak", and my name, to be precise, is Warden Willow. I like the name Willow, which, as you probably know, is another type of tree.'

He couldn't help but notice the blank faces on the animals, and he then pointed below him to a woody bump on the oak tree. 'Should you find one of those on an old oak tree, and you are in trouble—'

He didn't get chance to finish his sentence as Pal interrupted him. 'Oh, I know those! That's made by insects. It's called a gall, isn't it?'

The galoak nodded, and grinned. 'We have a wise dog here I can see! And as I was about to say, if you see a gall then you know a galoak, like myself, is in residence and will always be ready to help you.'

Pickle beamed at Pal. He was always very impressed with his friend's knowledge about so many different things, and he couldn't help but say to the little man, 'Pal is the most intelligent animal I have ever come across, Warden Willow!'

'Then Pickle, your friend here will be a great help in Harmony Haven when you get settled there. But look, we cannot talk here. You must come into my home and then you will know that you'll be safe. I am coming down now, so stand back all of you!'

Pal, Pickle and Patsy gasped together as they watched the galoak swing from branch to branch, high up in the tree above them, his arms extended to an unbelievable length, as if they were made of elastic. It was a very impressive display, and even more awesome when his arms stretched from the top of the trunk, all the way down to the ground and then returned to normal size—for a galoak—once again.

'Wow!' was the only exclamation made, as they were now able to see the little being properly for the first time, followed by Pal, adding 'You're amazing!' All the three friends were very impressed at Warden Willow.

'Come with me and stop staring!' the galoak laughed happily. 'I know I may look rather strange to you with my woody appearance!' He laughed again, as he looked at the newcomers that stood in front of him. 'But goodness me, you all look just as strange to me too!' He was laughing in a squeaky voice as he reached out and wiggled Pickle's curly tail, which made them all laugh together.

Suddenly Warden Willow stopped and looked thoughtful, as he had just remembered there was something he needed to do before he welcomed the newcomers into his home. He began to take a small bottle from a little pouch that was attached to his belt around his waist.

'I must do this important job before I do anything else,' he said, firmly. He then aimed the bottle towards the direction they had just walked through the wood, along the path. 'You'll find this amazing too!' he grinned at them, as he added, 'This will regrow all the under-growth that got broken as you made your way here—in superfast time!'

A fine spray shot from the bottle into the under-growth. Pickle, Pal and Patsy were very impressed at such a useful bottle that could repair broken branch-es, and they all watched and waited for something to happen. There was a rustling and movement in the woodland and then shoots appeared from the earth and broken branches healed themselves, just like the galoak had promised. But it was suddenly alarming that the broken branches were growing fast at a terrific pace towards them.

The galoak suddenly realised something was wrong, as all the plants and bushes were out of control and growing too fast. Instead of filling in the space they had come, the wood was growing towards them, closer and closer by the second.

'Into my home quick, all of you!' Warden Willow shouted, loudly. Then, to the friend's astonishment, he pushed open a hidden door in the trunk of the old oak tree and hurried them inside, as a rapidly growing tendril followed them inside...

CHAPTER 4

NATURE'S FEAST

The galoak slammed the door shut on the branch, breaking off the tip. 'Phew! That was strange!' he gasped. 'But you are all safe now,' he said with a weak laugh, as he tried to puzzle out what had gone wrong.

'Goodness me—that was a shock!' exclaimed Pickle.

'What, was that?' squealed Patsy.

'Yes, that was scary!' barked Pal.

The Woodland Warden rubbed his little head, a puzzled look on his face. 'I never expected that to happen. I cannot imagine what I did wrong.' And then the little man noticed the worried look of the newcomers. 'I am so sorry; please do not be afraid. This was not the welcome I wanted to give you, but we are all safe now.' He gave a laugh, 'I expect I'll have to cut my way out of my front door when I next use it now! What an amazing sight though... watching how fast those tendrils grew—phew!'

Pickle, Patsy and Pal soon relaxed now they were safely inside the home of the galoak. But they were surprised at what they were seeing there as they looked around the room inside of the oak tree.

'Well, looking at your faces, I can see you are all impressed with my home, which is called my billet. This is where I live when I am on duty, as I am at the moment. And as you can see, I have everything here that I need in the way of comfort,' said the galoak, proudly, with a wide smile, as he watched his visitors looking at so many items in the small room.

They excitedly inspected the bed, a chest of drawers and a wardrobe, which were all beautifully made of wood. They all noticed the small table and chairs, but there was something far more appealing to them as they saw, on top of the table, a wonderful sight—FOOD!

The Woodland Warden saw the delight in their eyes, as he said, warmly, 'Don't just look at it—this is for you! And it's all good food from the woodland. And you must try these biscuits. They were made by one of the rabbits in Harmony Haven. Expect them to be full of carrot, which rabbits love. So, tuck in my friends and enjoy your food.'

'We didn't expect all this, Warden Willow. Thank you for being so kind to us and it all looks wonderful,' said

Pal. 'We are extremely hungry, as we haven't eaten at all today, have we piglets...'

But the only reply that came was a 'Mmmm' from Patsy and Pickle, who already had their mouths full. But, they did nod their heads in agreement with the words Pal spoke. And the only sound in the room was the munching and crunching of food that was like a feast to the friends.

Patsy was casting her eyes around the home of the galoak. She liked the tiny pictures of butterflies and birds on the walls and sniffed with her snout at the vase of woodland flowers on the table, resisting a temptation to eat them, because they looked and smelt so nice. 'Your home is beautiful! It's so different from the pig-sties that we lived in,' she said dreamily. 'I would really love to have a home like this.' She suddenly stopped talking, as she noticed how quickly the other two were eating. Soon there would be nothing left for her if she didn't stop talking, so she soon got eating again.

'I appreciate your kind words,' replied Warden Wil-low, with a smile. He was enjoying seeing the food he had provided was being eaten with such gusto. 'Now I expect you are all in need of a drink after your tiring walk—and eating so much!'

He stretched out an arm to reach a shelf that was very high above him. He grinned as he heard them all gasp as they looked up from eating to see his arm stretch up getting longer and longer as it did so. From the shelf he took down three wooden bowls and asked kindly, 'What would you like now. I have made juices from apples, rose hips and blackberries. Or, if you prefer, there is water.'

'This is so nice being asked what we would like to drink,' said Pickle. 'Usually we have dirty rainwater, which we can drink, of course, but it's lovely to have a choice! I think I am going to like our new life very much.' Pickle grunted in joy.

'I'd just like water please,' said Pal, who was feeling quite emotional about the kindness that was being shown to them by this strange little character, who obviously had a very big kind-loving heart.

'May I try the rose hip juice, please,' said Patsy gently, although she had only ever tasted water and her mother's milk when she was small. She quite fancied something different on this very amazing day. 'We certainly are being spoilt and it's a very nice feeling,' she added.

'And what would you like Pickle?' enquired the galoak.

Pickle was taking longer to decide as he couldn't make up his mind. 'I quite like apples, so I would love some apple juice, please.' He glanced quickly at his friends, before adding, 'Would you think me very greedy if I asked if I could try them all? After all, this is a very special day!'

'You are so greedy Pickle!' grunted Patsy, and Pal barked in agreement. Although, Patsy had clearly forgotten that, between the three of them, they had eaten all of the food and not a single crumb was left on the table. Warden Willow laughed in a squeaky laugh to himself. He knew that pigs were known to be intelligent and friendly, and Pickle had just confirmed that he really was a 'greedy pig' as well.

The friends all watched with interest as Warden Willow poured the juices from various bottles into the two bowls. He then opened up a small cupboard in the wall of the tree. They saw water dripping into a barrel below. Then, turning a small tap on the barrel, he carefully filled another bowl with water for Pal.

'This is water from a natural stream, Pal, and it will help you keep up your strength. And you enjoy the juices, Patsy and Pickle, as you have still got a way to walk, but at least you can take your time now, knowing that you are safe from danger.' The galoak felt happy as he watched them all drink and then lick their lips. Now they were looking more relaxed as they settled themselves onto a rag-made rug on the floor.

'I know I am going to love our new life. It is very exciting to experience a different way of life,' said Patsy cheerfully, as she rolled on the rug, finding its comfort very enjoyable indeed. In fact, after all the tasty food and drink, she felt like taking a nap.

'You have been so kind to us Warden Willow,' said Pickle gratefully, as he gave Patsy a nudge, noticing her eyes getting sleepy. 'We really do appreciate your kindness. We were on the verge of starvation because we got very little to eat on the farm.' Pickle looked apologetic, and guilty. 'And if I have appeared greedy, I am so sorry but everything you gave us has been so delicious.'

'Well, I'm just glad I have been able to help and it's nice to see you all looking better,' grinned the Woodland Warden. 'Maybe we should all rest a bit before we go on our way,' he laughed, looking at Patsy on her belly, trying to keep her eyes open. 'I can see one little piggy is ready for bed!'

Patsy smiled, as her eyes closed. Soon she was snoring away. Pickle and Pal chuckled, and the Woodland Warden joined in.

'Let's sit here and get to know each other better, while she rests,' said Warden Willow. 'I would love to know more about you, and I expect you all feel the same about me.'

'That's a good idea! A rest and a chat would be very nice,' agreed Pal. 'And I would like to know if you live in this billet all the time?'

'No, my real home is in one of the Outer-Lands of Harmony Haven,' he replied in his squeaky voice. 'I live with all the other galoaks there. We have families too.' He gave a deep sigh before speaking again. 'You know each of you will find your new home, a truly amazing and wonderful place to live in, but everyone, even myself, has a part to play to help Oliver Gruffle keep it that way. We are all part of a big happy family, no matter what we are or where we have come from. We are just so lucky to have Oliver as our guardian, to care for us and see that we all live a good life.'

'I just feel so excited listening to you,' Pickle said in a joyful voice. 'And I can't wait to meet Oliver Gruffle.'

'Nor can I!' agreed Pal. The dog then looked serious as he asked the Woodland Warden, 'May I ask what your life is like?'

The little galoak nodded and stood up and stretched

himself as tall as he could. 'We galoaks are proud to be part of the Harmony Haven Home Guard,' he said with pride. 'We patrol the woodlands, waiting for new-comers like yourselves, so we can show you the way to safety. But listen, that's enough talk about me!' He glanced at Pal before saying, 'Tell me Pal, how did you come to meet Scrumpy? He must have realised you were in need of help to tell you about Harmony Haven.'

Pal wagged his tail at the thought of talking about his lovable friend Scrumpy. 'We cannot express how very grateful we are to him for helping us come to a safe and better life. He will always be a very dear friend to us all.'

'Good little Scrumpy!' Pickle squealed, so loudly it woke Patsy.

She yawned, got up and said, 'Where's Scrumpy?!'

Everybody laughed and then the Woodland Warden gave them a gentle smile of agreement. 'We haven't met Scrumpy yet, so come on Pal, tell us about him, as we can't wait to know more about him.'

The two piglets sat attentively in front of Pal, waiting to hear his story. They reminded Warden Willow of his own children, Cedar and Teak, who would love to hear him tell stories. *Families are all the same*, he thought to himself. *We all love the comfort of each other, no matter who or what we are.*

CHAPTER 5

SCRUMPY THE MOONLING

When Pal had everyone's attention, as requested by the Woodland Warden, he began his story about how he came to meet this very special little man, known as Scrumpy.

'It was a cold night; the wind was blowing and the rain pouring down and making huge puddles in the farmyard. And I felt as miserable as can be just sitting in my run-down kennel and wishing for a happier life. When in the farmyard, near to my kennel, I heard a different noise. I thought to myself, maybe it was a fox or even a badger searching for food, so I looked out to see what the noise was. Knowing the farmer and his family had already gone to bed, as I had seen the lights in the farmhouse go out. I was amazed to see a small chubby person, stamping his feet as if trying to keep warm. I noticed that he was soaked through, and that he was not a human child. I felt so sorry for him looking so cold and wet.'

'If he wasn't a human child, then what was he?' asked Patsy, curiously.

Pal laughed at her impatience. 'Don't rush me Patsy, you'll find out in a minute!' Patsy snorted, impatiently but quieted down seeing Pal was staring at her, before continuing, 'So, I watched him for a short while and then I shouted to him, "You're very welcome to share my kennel with me if you would like to come in out of the rain!" And I was quite shocked when he accepted my offer. He told me his name was Scrumpy, and I told him my name was Pal. And we instantly became friends. But he did laugh when he noticed I was staring at him, which I suppose was rather rude. And then he told me a story that I could hardly believe!'

'I love a good story and I'm loving this one Pal,' said Pickle in an excited voice.

Pal then turned to Warden Willow and said, 'Did you know, Scrumpy's ancestors came from the moon!'

'WHAT!? Are you kidding us?' Pickle blurted, before the Warden could reply. 'Did they jump off the moon to reach here?' he squealed, causing laughter amongst them all.

'Yes Pal,' Warden Willow replied. 'Actually, I did know Scrumpy was known as a "moonling" and where his family once came from. And Pickle, I also can tell you the moon is far, far away and impossible for anyone to jump off and land here on Earth.'

'Oh,' replied Pickle feeling rather silly. 'Anyway, I suppose the man in the moon would stop anyone doing that anyway.'

Pal laughed as he heard his friend's remarks. 'I'll tell you shortly how his ancestors reached here—it's an amazing story!' The Border collie glanced at the galoak and was glad to see he was smiling with enjoyment at the tale he was telling. He turned to the piglets and continued his tale: 'Scrumpy told me his ancestors were a peaceful, happy community who lived in caverns deep inside the moon. They had everything they needed for survival—even water and edible cheese bugs that lived inside of rocks,' said Pal matter-of-factly. 'But then their lives were disrupted by an increase in the number of moonquakes, which would send tremors throughout their homes, sending rocks falling all around them.'

'You certainly had some very interesting chats with Scrumpy, Pal and, if I might add, you tell a good story my friend,' praised the galoak with a smile, who admired this very wise dog.

'And what happened next?' asked Pickle once again.

'Well,' Pal said, 'previously, when they saw a crack

developing in the walls of their homes, they would repair it with a filler. But, they found they were losing the battle against the moonquakes and many of the little people were being killed or badly injured by the danger that was all around them.'

'That must have been very scary for them,' said Patsy in a caring way.

'It was,' nodded Pal. 'Scrumpy told me, the "Wise-Ones" made a very important decision for the community. These Wise-Ones were highly intelligent leaders and who decided on important matters. And they decided that some of their community should be sent on a moon craft to Earth to try and save their race, which, sadly, was diminishing every day.'

'It was an amazing thing to do,' said Warden Willow, in a serious voice. 'Sorry Pal, I didn't mean to interrupt!'

Pal smiled at the galoak, before saying, 'It appears that, when the moon craft circled the Earth, to find a place to land, they spotted the Isle of Wight—an Island that looked green and lush, and just right for a secret landing! And so, this is why the Island became the moonling's home.'

'You mean, Scrumpy's ancestors on the Island were

Aliens!?' gasped Pickle. 'Just like the story you told me not so long ago, Pal!'

Pal laughed, remembering scaring the life out of the little piglet when he told him that he hoped that if Aliens ever came to Earth, they wouldn't be meat eaters! But then that was before he had met Scrumpy. And Pickle had said to him, it seemed as if he was in a losing position with his life, because most humans loved meat, and if the aliens did too, he was doomed to be in someone's tummy.

The piglets and Warden Willow listened in silence again after Pal coughed to get their attention. 'Scrumpy told me later that his ancestors made another decision: to move into Harmony Haven with Oliver Gruffle. It was a very happy move for them all, because they could be together in a small village of their own, and help Oliver by being able to build homes, do other jobs and gather food to help the community.'

'And,' added Warden Willow. 'Oliver knows his job as Protector and Guardian of Harmony Haven would have been much harder without the support of these fun-loving little people!'

'What was Scrumpy doing on the Island then, if he lives in Harmony Haven?' asked Pickle curiously.

'Good question,' replied Pal. 'Well, in many ways this will tell us all about the kind nature of these little people. Scrumpy told me his ancestors delighted in keeping the Island beautiful for future generations. They picked up litter and planted bulbs along the hedgerows—which was what Scrumpy was up to that night—for everyone to enjoy when they flower.'

The galoak then added, 'Yes Pal, but we mustn't forget, as well as looking after the Island, all the time these little people are on the lookout for animals and birds that need a safe place to live, and as we all know, that is Harmony Haven.'

Patsy was amazed at all she was hearing and said gently, 'I am really looking forward to meeting Scrumpy and saying thank you.'

'Me too!' added Pickle.

Pal looked at his friend. 'And you think I am wise, but Scrumpy and I would spend many hours together just talking. He taught me so much about so many different things, so I have him to thank for sharing his knowledge with me.'

Warden Willow then laughed knowingly as he said, 'Yes Pal, but I'm just glad he hasn't taught you how to play tricks on others. He has caught me out many times, but I'm much wiser now about his mischief, so I won't get caught out again!'

Pal then spoke, once the laughter had died down, in a serious voice. 'Then one night, Scrumpy noticed I was limping, quite badly, and I told him I had been ill-treated and I wanted to run away from the farm and take my dear friends here with me. And then I heard Farmer Muggleton wanted to make sausages with his pigs, so we had no time to lose!'

Pal smiled gently at the piglets. 'Of course, I, like most animals, had heard of Harmony Haven—a place of safety. And Oliver Gruffle was the Guardian, but I thought it was just a fairy story that had been passed down through families and friends. So, it was quite a shock to learn Scrumpy knew how to get there and finding out it was where he lived!' The Border collie then become very excited as he added, 'He told me the secret way and that we would have to look out for our first guide, the Woodland Warden, and so here we are, safe and sound!'

The galoak looked happily around the group of friends and felt a great joy inside, as he saw their happiness shining in their eyes. But he also knew that being able to help others was indeed very rewarding to himself as well. He then rose from his chair, stretched and said, 'We have spent a long time resting and talking so I think we should be on our way now.'

The piglets and Pal all looked at the smiling face of the Woodland Warden, each wondering what the next part of their journey would bring. But something seemed wrong, because Warden Willow was standing, motionless, with wide open eyes and a look of disbelieve on his face. And then to the friend's amazement he started to laugh and laugh and laugh. So much so, he curled over, holding his tummy.

Pal, Pickle and Patsy watched him, each wearing a weak smile on their faces, as they wondered what could be so funny to cause such a reaction from the little woody man.

'I am so stupid!' he suddenly blurted out. 'I've just realised why the branches in the wood suddenly grew towards us, instead of growing in the direction you had all just come. It was that cheeky, Scrumpy! I'm sure of it! He got the spray for me and—I hate to admit it—but he's caught me out with one of his pranks again! He must have slipped me the wrong one. I should have read the label—oh dear!' He then burst into laughter again, 'Just wait 'till I get my hands on him!'

Now they all laughed with him, and even more so

when Pal added, with a grin, 'And you thought you would never get caught out by him again!'

Warden Willow nodded his head and continued chuckling to himself about the incident.

Then the three friends agreed that this had turned into a wonderful, happy day with the galoak. They hadn't laughed so much in a very long time and realised that Scrumpy, for all his mischief, was a very dear friend to have. Judging by the chuckling that was coming from Warden Willow, he had forgiven him already.

CHAPTER 6

STOP, LOOK AND LISTEN!

Warden Willow was still laughing, as he made his way to another door that was at the back of the tree room. But before he could open it, Pal was having one of his wise moments. Something had been puzzling him for quite a while.

'Warden Willow, may I ask you a question before we go? Am I correct in thinking we have entered some kind of magical world? Because I'm thinking, logically, how is it possible to get furniture and all your belongings into the trunk of this oak tree, and still have room to spare?'

'What's magical mean, Pal?' quizzed Pickle, who was not as worldly as his friend.

But Pal was waiting for the reply from the galoak. But all he got was a wink from the little man, so he and the piglets were none the wiser.

'Come on now, no time for chatter anymore!' said Warden Willow. 'We must be on our way!'

The galoak opened the back door of his tree home and beckoned for them to follow him. And much to the delight of the friends, the opening revealed, not bushes and undergrowth that can scratch badly, but an open woodland, which had plenty of trees to walk between quite easily.

'Follow me,' Warden Willow said cheerily, as he closed the door to his billet. And then he marched ahead with his head held high.

Pal, Pickle and Patsy laughed as they followed behind him, trying their best to march in the same manner, which was not so easy for them—with four legs each! Then after a while he changed his step to a run, and now and then, checking behind him, to make sure the newcomers were keeping up with him, and smiling with his happy face at them. The animal friends laughed as the little man cheekily started dancing around them, grinning as he urged them to do the same, while he darted in and out between them. And the three friends could feel his happiness inside of them, as they too joined in with the dancing. They all had a feeling of such joy, as they happily danced around each other, and they all felt something they had not known for a very long time. Pal gave a yap and the piglets grunted to the tune of the little man as he started singing and clapping wildly.

'Are you always this happy?' laughed Pickle, in a curious voice.

The galoak grinned widely as he replied to the question. 'Happy? Why, yes! I'm always happy. Just look around us. What do you see?'

'Trees, trees and more trees!' answered Patsy as she swirled around Pickle, her eyes wide with excitement. She had never danced before and was finding the experience very enjoyable and relaxing.

The galoak tutted. 'STOP!—All of you! Just stand still. STOP, LOOK and LISTEN!' He said firmly.

The friends did as he requested and wondered why he had insisted they stop dancing, because they had been enjoying it so much. But now they listened with interest to what the little man was saying. He pointed out the various birds as they flew in and out of the branches of the trees. They watched birds pick at the red berries, and seeds and insects. The Woodland Warden could tell what the bird was, just by listening to it sing, and he explained what each was called to the interested friends. Apart from Pal knowing what an oak tree looked like, thanks to Scrumpy describing it to him, none of them knew the names of each type of tree either, until the Warden Willow pointed out the various tree leaf shapes to help them identify them. They noticed a fallen tree, and he then explained that the rings on the trunk showed just how old that tree was. They learned that it grew a new ring for every year of its life. They gasped as a mouse scurried by in front of them, just stopping for a brief second to gaze at the group, before scurrying away out of sight. The galoak then pointed through the trees to a fox, laying on the ground in the autumn sun that shined through the branches out of the trees. The fox had a brightly coloured red coat and a bushy tail. And each of them realised that they certainly were enjoying what the Woodland Warden had told them to do: Stop, Look and Listen!

The galoak then pointed to the ground. 'Tell me, what do you see?' he asked happily, as he saw the delight on the faces of the newcomers.

'I see earth and more earth!' grunted Pickle, as he contentedly snuffled under a pile of leaves.

'That is what is wrong with this world,' the galoak replied. 'We are given eyes to see, ears to hear, but we don't use them like we should! We live on such a beautiful Island that we should take time to enjoy all the beauty that is around us everywhere.'

'There are lots of acorns,' said Patsy, keenly, as she hoped to impress the galoak with her observation.

'Yes, Patsy, you are correct,' said Warden Willow with delight. 'And did you know that, below the surface of the earth, there are bulbs and flowers just waiting to grow in the springtime. Then the woodlands will be filled with colour from bluebells, snowdrops, daffodils, wood anemones and primroses everywhere. And they will all set our hearts a-flutter with their beauty!'

He then went on to explain in detail what the flowers would look like and the colours of the petals. He also pointed out the mosses and ferns growing in the damp darker areas. Together they studied oak apples and marvelled at the wild berries that grew on the bushes and trees. He showed them the fungi that grew on some of the trees, and pointed out mushrooms and toadstools, but warned that many of these were poisonous and should never be touched or eaten. They all crouched low as a bee, laden with pollen on its legs, swooped just a bit too close to them. After it had flown away, the little man went on to explain that the bee would take its pollen back to its hive. The bee colony would use it to make honey, which he explained was so sweet and tasty and very good to eat. The friends were filled with delight at the sight of a red admiral butterfly making the most of its short life as autumn fell upon them. And how they laughed together, as a cheeky red robin, with a bright red breast, walked his territory, searching for worms.

'Who wouldn't be happy living on our beautiful Island!' said the galoak happily to the three friends, who had listened and seen so many interesting things that they clearly hadn't noticed in detail before.

'We agree,' said Pal, nodding. 'I think I would love to be able to teach others like you have done to us this morning.'

'That's good to hear Pal. I am sure that teaching others would be gratefully appreciated by Oliver Gruffle. It is a good feeling to be able to pass on knowledge to others—and we are never too old to learn!'

'I have really enjoyed watching the butterflies,' said Patsy, happily. 'In future, I am certainly going to "Stop, Look and Listen!" no matter where I am!'

'And me too!' added Pickle, seriously. 'I find it very weird that we see with our eyes and yet we miss things that are right in front of us—until someone like Warden Willow takes the time to point them out!' Pickle couldn't help feeling as wise as Pal with his own comments, and he grew in stature as the little man told him how wise he sounded.

So, the happy group of friends, along with Warden Willow went on their way, delighting in everything that was being told to them about the woodlands. And as they listened and walked peacefully in amongst the trees, plants and birds, they found a new feeling was entering their bodies; the unhappiness of living on the farm was gradually leaving them, now replaced with joyfulness.

And the little wooden man smiled to himself, for he knew he had played his part in making sure they began their new life with happiness in their hearts.

CHAPTER 7

THE GALOAK'S ADVICE

As they continued to walk through the woodlands, the little galoak suddenly stopped, and told them, rather sadly, that they were nearly at the next part of their journey, and it would soon be time for him to leave them. The friends all knew they would be sorry to say goodbye to this new friend, who had been so kind to them and taught them so much. They smiled at each other, and then watched in amazement when he stretched his long arm high up into a branch on a tree above, to feed a berry to a small bird. Not only had he been kind to them, but he was kind to all living creatures in the woodland.

Walking a short distance more, Warden Willow stopped again and said, with a deep sigh, 'Well, my dear friends, here we are. It's time for you to go on the next stage of your journey with a new guide.' He then gazed kindly at them. 'Do you know what else makes me happy?' he said. 'It is making new friends! We will meet again soon. Maybe once you are all settled you would like to visit my real home. My family would make you very welcome. But for now, I wish you all a happiness in Harmony Haven. I have enjoyed being your guide for now.'

He extended his long arms around them in a farewell hug. A sadness fell over the three friends as they said their goodbyes to this dear little man.

He once again said, 'And always remember what I told you… to Stop, Look, and Listen!'

They all nodded and promised.

And then he added seriously, 'And that includes, when you cross a road too!'

Pal looked at the galoak with a puzzled look, whilst Pickle and Patsy knew the only road they had ever crossed was the one they had followed Pal on, earlier that morning, into the woodlands. But the little man was quick to remind them when he saw their puzzled faces. 'Do you remember when you crossed the road to come into the woodland? You all ran across the road! And not one of you stopped, looked or listened!' He tutted as he looked at the three friends.

Pal was even more puzzled. 'We will remember your words, Warden Willow. But how did you know we had run across the road without looking—when you weren't even there?'

Warden Willow scratched his wooden forehead and looked at Pal in the same puzzled way. 'Do you know, Pal, I don't really know!' He gave a chuckle. 'It could be magic, or it could be those little blue birds flying above us now who whispered it into my ear?'

And sure enough, when the three friends looked up, they all gasped at the delightful sight of the little birds flying in a circle above them, their blue bodies, quite unlike any small bird they had ever seen before.

'Aren't they delightful,' said Patsy, who was charmed by them. The only other birds she had really noticed were the black-feathered rooks, crows and blackbirds that hung around the farm in a menacing way.

'Now my dear friends, it's time you were all on your way,' the galoak said softly. 'I shall stay here and watch you until you meet up with your new guide.'

He then pointed towards a nearby mound with a small dark tunnel entrance. 'That is where you will meet up with him. He's called Mr Dozer. He is a badger and, I'm sorry to say, he has a reputation for being bit boring and grumpy, so please don't fall asleep out of boredom!'

'We will try not to,' answered Pickle, chuckling. But

then he felt sad. 'We will miss you Warden Willow. It's been so nice spending time with you.'

'We will meet again soon,' replied Warden Willow. 'This is not goodbye, forever. Oh, by the way, I must give you all a bit of advice. Never mention the word "MAGIC" to the guardian, Oliver Gruffle.'

'Why?' queried the three friends, in one voice.

'Oh, you'll find out!' And then with another chuckle, he stretched out his long arms and sprung up into the nearest tree, vanishing out of sight.

'Goodbye Warden Willow and thank you for your kindness to us,' shouted Pal, but Warden Willow had disappeared.

'Wasn't he amazing!' said Pickle.

Pal and Patsy nodded their heads in agreement. They all felt sad at his departure, but happy inside knowing that one day they would meet him again, because they had made a kindly new friend.

'Come on you two,' said Pal excitedly. 'Let's go and meet our next guide and continue on our journey. Do you both feel glad that you came with me?'

'Happy? I'm more than happy!' laughed Pickle.

'Me too!' added Patsy. 'But Pal, if this badger is going

to be so grumpy, I don't think the next part of our journey is going to be so enjoyable, do you?'

'Well, we must judge Mr Dozer for ourselves,' said Pal. 'We can't all be the same, and besides, do you remember how we all felt at the farm? Miserable and unhappy! And just look at us now! We are all filled with happiness!'

The piglets laughed loudly, as they watched Pal twirling around and barking loudly, 'I'm so happy! Yes, I am! Happy! Happy! Happy!'

And then they joined him too until they tired and could dance no more.

Suddenly they heard laughing coming from a nearby tree and they knew the Woodland Warden was still watching over them.

'I think we should be on our way, over to the mound now,' said Pal, as he urged the pigs forward with his muzzle.

'Stop that Pal! Can't you see we are pigs, not sheep! You don't have to round us up,' grunted Pickle. 'And by the way, who were you posting letters too yesterday? I'm dying to know!'

'I'll explain about the letters when I'm ready, Pickle, but not now!' insisted Pal, barking again at them to move. 'Let's go and meet Mr Dozer.' Pal pushed at Pickle with his nose. 'Lead the way young piggy! Left-right! Left-right! Just like the Woodland Warden showed us.'

Patsy frowned as she watched her beloved Pickle marching. 'You don't march like that Pickle! Why are you wriggling your bottom from side-to-side?'

Pickle turned to look at the two animals, who meant so much to him, and said, cheekily, 'My body is full of happiness and sunshine as well. But, I confess, with all the great food we were given, I was quite greedy and it's making me—parp!'

'PICKLE! You are so rude!' said Pal.

'Serves you right for being greedy!' squealed Patsy, giggling. 'But we still love you!'

And then they laughed even longer when they heard the Woodland Warden join in, his laugh echoing in the trees far behind them.

'We have to be the luckiest animals around today, my dear friends,' said Pal thoughtfully, as they walked on towards the mound. 'And think of all the exciting adventures we will have in Harmony Haven!'

'I'm sure you will!' shouted the Woodland Warden, as he watched them, from high up in the trees behind them. 'And remember what I said newcomers—please never mention the word "MAGIC" to Oliver Gruffle!'

The three friends waved back but they still couldn't see him in the trees, and then the woodland filled with the happy sound of birds singing and squirrels scurrying across the leaf-strewn ground. And above them flew the pretty blue birds again, as if they were keeping a watchful eye on the animals.

As Pal, Pickle and Patsy now looked forward to the next part of their journey, each of them was thinking to themselves, how lucky they were to be given this chance for a brighter and happier life in Harmony Haven, and to have someone to love and care for them forever—the mysterious, Oliver Gruffle!

When they reached the mound, the friends smiled at each other, knowing that a new adventure on their journey was about to begin...

CHAPTER 8

GLOOM AND DOOM

'I do hope that Mr Dozer will be a nice badger,' said Patsy.

They stood in front of the mound that the Woodland Warden had told them to go to.

'There's no sign of anyone here at all,' said Pal, curiously, as he looked around. 'I know this mound is called a badger's sett—or burrow, so he's probably under the ground. Shall we all shout his name together, so he knows we are here?'

Together the three friends all peered into the dark hole in the mound, and then, as loud as they could, they shouted, 'Mr Dozer! We are the newcomers! Are you home?'

There came a noise from below and a voice shouted back to them, 'Alright, alright! I'm coming! And you can stop making that awful noise. You made me jump in my sleep!'

Pal, Patsy and Pickle exchanged glances, as they waited for their new guide, who sounded like a rather grumpy badger, judging by the way he had spoken to them.

All their eyes were on him as he climbed out of the hole and said, 'I would like to inform you that I am a Grand Master at creating tunnels and it is a great honour for you to be allowed to step inside my sett. I can see that it's obvious that none of you are badgers!'

Pal looked the badger directly in his eyes. 'Thank you, Mr Dozer. We are really looking forward to having you as our guide—and yes, we all feel honoured, deeply honoured to be meeting such a distinguished gentleman.' Pal winked at Pickle and Patsy. They knew he was putting on his Border collie charm.

The badger appeared to be startled by Pal's kind words, flattered almost, as he looked the newcomers over. While the badger was speechless, Pal decided this was a good time for him to introduce himself and the two piglets.

They all then stared at the badger who was standing in front of them, as he brushed down the orange jacket that he was wearing and tightened the string that was holding up his trousers. The friends had seen many badgers before on the farm at night-time, but never one that was wearing clothes, and one wearing spectacles perched on his nose. But what was so strange to them also was that he was standing upright on his two back legs and could walk without falling over.

Whilst they watched Mr Dozer scratching his head and yawning, the badger suddenly spoke to them in a sleepy way. 'Don't any of you know what it means when an animal is nocturnal?' His voice got more grumpier as he added bluntly, 'It means I sleep during the day and come out at night to do my work and eat. What is the point of being nocturnal if I am rudely woken up at this hour!'

The trio were a bit put out, and then Pickle replied, 'We are very sorry Mr Dozer,' said Pickle in an apologetic voice. 'The Woodland Warden said you would be our guide and ready to help us now.'

The badger nodded his head in a knowing kind of way. 'Huh! The Woodland Warden! And I suppose he told you all about the wonderful things in the woodland.' The friends thought he sounded rather sarcastic about the Woodland Warden, as he continued to speak. 'Did he tell you about adders that crawl along the ground, a nasty snake that can bite you! And mushrooms and fungi that some of them are poisonous if eaten. Huh! Yes, and what about the birds with their dirty habits! If you'll excuse me talking rudely—that "poop" on your head!' He then added grimly, 'It all sounds blooming awful, the woodland, to me, but I suppose you all found it very interesting and had a wonderful time with the very interesting Woodland Warden! Huh!'

Pal, Patsy and Pickle could only nod their heads in agreement, as they were quite amazed at how outspoken the badger was, and they didn't want to upset him further, because he was the same size as themselves, standing upright. And they didn't like the way he was cleaning his long sharp-looking claws either.

'Well, you are with me now,' Mr Dozer huffed. 'And I can tell you, it's all gloom and doom down there in the tunnels and far from interesting!' The badger looked as if he couldn't care what they thought of him. 'And I expect you were told I'm just a grumpy old badger, with a "chip on my shoulder", as they say, because no one seems to like me—huh! Well, that's just what I am, and that's how I'm going to stay—so you three will just have to put up with me!'

Pal could see the badger was extremely grumpy and quite rude, but he really wanted to show him they were friends. 'Sir,' he said respectfully, 'I'm sure we will find your world just as interesting as the woodland.'

The badger's eyes widened with interest as he looked

at Pal. 'Did you call me "Sir", young man?' he exclaimed in astonishment. It had been a long time since anyone had shown him such respect.

'Yes, Sir, I did, because as a "Grand Master" of creating tunnels, you clearly deserve respect. After all, I can only dig the smallest of holes to hide a bone, and my friends are certainly no good at digging either—' Pickle and Patsy looked a little annoyed at this, and they were about to say so, when Pal shot back a look at them, as if to say 'Shhh, I'm working my "puppy-dog eyes" charm!'

The badger eagerly watched Pal, enjoying being praised. 'Please, continue, Pal...'

Pal looked back at the badger. 'I was about to say that you can also walk and stand on your two back legs—and that is just amazing! We have met lots of badgers before and none of them are as clever as you!'

Mr Dozer grinned. 'Well I never!' he added, nodding his head with approval, and delighted with the words that this charming dog had spoken to him. 'Thank you, Pal, for your kind words. You flatter me! At last someone with some old-fashioned respect!'

Pal winked at his friends and grinned widely, because he knew they would be thinking to themselves, 'Pal, you're such a creep!'

After a silence of a few minutes, whilst the badger nodded to himself in a knowing way and looked quite pleased with what had been said about him, the three friends were shocked when he suddenly reverted to his rude manner and said, as he eyed Pickle and Patsy, 'I see we have two piglets here with rather large bottoms!'

Pal felt this was a very rude thing to say about his friends, and wanted to growl at him, but decided to keep quiet, because they were depending on him to be their next guide. But Pickle felt an urge to push the badger over with his snout, but Pal whispered in Pickle's ear to just ignore the comments.

Mr Dozer then exclaimed in a bad-tempered way, seeming to completely forget that Pal had spoken to him in a respectful manner just a moment ago. 'I want to inform you, Pal, that dogs and myself have had a few battles in the past on the Island when they have invaded my various homes. But, fortunately, not here in Harmony Haven, where we are all equals—thank goodness! But as you have not yet taken your vows before Oliver Gruffle, to be a kind animal and be respectful to all, I'm warning you, doggy, one nip from you and my tunnels will become your worst nightmare! Do I make myself clear or do I need to repeat my warning?'

Pal's tail drooped between his legs, as he nodded

his head, while stifling a growl. He so wanted to bark at the badger for being rude. How very different this badger was compared to the kind and caring nature of the Woodland Warden.

Of course, Pickle had great admiration for Pal and his wisdom, but he also wanted to show Patsy that he could be as bold as Pal, to defend his dear friend, who wasn't looking bold at the moment. 'Mr Dozer,' said Pickle, firmly. 'Pal is my dearest friend, and he would never hurt anyone. He's a kind, loving dog and a great friend to have. And it is thanks to his caring nature that Patsy and I were rescued from a terrible fate. I'm sorry to say this but *you* are in the wrong to judge Pal when you don't even know him!' Pickle then gave a loud 'Oink!' to let the badger know he was very annoyed.

Pal smiled weakly at his friend but wished Pickle had kept his words to himself as he feared the badger would refuse to help them.

'And he's polite too!' said Patsy in a bold voice, still fuming inside about the remark made about their large bottoms—which *she* thought were perfect! And she couldn't resist adding, 'We haven't judged you!' she said firmly with a slight smile, 'Although, we were told you would be grumpy!'

Pal barked, hoping that the badger had not heard Patsy's words, truly hoping the badger would still be their guide.

Mr Dozer peered over the top of his spectacles that were perched at the end of his nose. He frowned for a moment and then shook his head. 'Well, we can't stand here chatting anymore,' Mr Dozer said, his tone changing to a kinder manner. 'It's time we were on our way.' He then lifted out a pile of white garments from inside his sett. 'I will help you put these capes on, which will protect you from getting bruised because there will be loose earth falling on your head in the tunnels.'

After the badger had helped them all put on the capes, the three friends actually laughed at themselves as they looked at each other, because this was the first time they had ever worn an item of clothing and it felt very strange indeed and difficult to walk in as well.

Mr Dozer gave a weak smile when he saw the newcomers were all laughing at how they looked. And they laughed at him as well, when he put the cape over the top of his clothes.

'We look like ghosts—woooohhh!' said Pal as he began to act silly in front of his friends. He knew all about ghosts, because Scrumpy had told him about all the haunted places on the Island.

'What are ghosts, Pal?' asked Pickle curiously, eager to learn all he could from his friend, as he hoped that one day he would be as wise as him.

'Ghosts are like... if Farmer Muggleton ran over a hedgehog and killed it, and then the eerie vision of a hedgehog coming back would be a ghost,' explained Pal. 'And ghosts like to scare others by going "Wooh! Wooh!"'

Pickle and Patsy laughed as Pal balanced on his hind legs and pretended to scare them.

But the badger was thinking to himself as he watched the newcomers having fun—*why is it that every animal and being appears to be happy, but not me?* But something else was troubling him as well, as he remembered only a short while ago, that he had explained to the three friends that when they take their vows before Oliver Gruffle, they had to promise they would be kind and respectful to others. And he knew he had not been very friendly towards them and had forgotten about the vows he had made, so very long ago.

Talking in a friendlier voice, Mr Dozer said, 'Now, about your bottoms... Because they are quite rounded and large, there is no way you can use the tunnel in my sett. But follow me to my emergency tunnel instead.'

The piglets grunted again at the comment, but Pal nudged them on. Before long, Mr Dozer stopped and jumped up and down on a grassy area, and then peered close to the ground, as if he was searching for a lost item.

Pal whispered to the piglets. 'Badgers have very poor eyesight, but I think he must be looking for his emergency tunnel—or a worm for his dinner!' he chuckled. 'But, perhaps we shouldn't judge Mr Dozer about being bad-tempered, because, when I first wake up, I often feel grumpy too, and of course he is a nocturnal animal, so is most awake at night. So, I suppose we should be grateful that he has got out of bed in the daytime to help us on our journey.'

The piglets smiled at Pal and nodded.

'I've found it!' shouted badger, eventually, in a relieved tone of voice. And then with his paws he started to tug on a large section of grass, and then a wooden trap door was revealed leading into a deep dark hole, sloping down into further tunnels below.

The badger noted the nervous looks on the faces of the newcomers as they peered into the blackness.

His voice softened, reassuring them, 'You mustn't be afraid. You can trust me, because, as I have told you, I am a Grand Master at creating tunnels! And believe me, Oliver Gruffle would never have entrusted you to me, if he did not think I was capable of looking after you all safely.' He smiled at them all kindly.

Pal, Pickle and Patsy all gave a loud sigh of relief and then they all listened carefully to what the badger was telling them, as he explained what they would see below, and what he wanted them to do. He made it clear they must obey him at all times, because the tunnels were his territory. The badger then told them that the entrance to this tunnel was on a small slope, so they could slide down quite easily—on their rather large bottoms! He had placed dried grass at the end of the slope, so they would have a soft landing. Mr Dozer also reassured them that the tunnels would be bright and well-lit by lanterns, so there was no need to feel afraid, because all they would encounter were tree roots, worms and a few harmless insects.

Pal then lead the way, followed by Patsy and Pickle. Mr Dozer came last because he had to close the trap door of the emergency tunnel. But he also knew, being last, the piglets would make a nice bouncy landing for him—if he happened to land on top of them!

The friends all giggled in delight as they slid down the slope, but in their ears they heard Mr Dozer mumble. 'We are on our way now, down into the doom and gloom—with grumpy old badger!'

CHAPTER 9

THE INVADERS

Following after Pal, the two piglets headed into the tunnels. They found it very scary entering this strange underground place that was dark and smelt of dampness. But then they heard Pal shout back that he had safely reached the bottom of the slope and encouraged them not to be scared. So, the two piglets nervously followed after Pal, and were soon joined by the badger.

'Now, that wasn't so bad was it?' said Mr Dozer, but not waiting for a reply, he set about lighting more lanterns that were attached to wooden beams on the walls.

Pal, Patsy and Pickle looked around and were glad that now they could see more clearly, and it wasn't so dark. But as none of them had ever been below ground before, they still found this a very frightening experience. As the friends looked around, they could see tree roots of all shapes and sizes, twisting and winding their way downwards, deep into the ground below. Some of the roots were huge and must have belonged to very large old trees. They watched with interest as earthworms, some small and others long and fat, tunnelled into the earth. And they all gasped as Mr Dozer made a lunch of quite a few. Their eyes widened as they watched strange-looking insects creep along the tunnels, minding their own business and not heeding the newcomers or the badger. Busy ants scurried along the tunnels, carrying with them, bits of food and eggs they had laid, all in line, like an army, as they marched past the onlookers, ignoring them completely. Spiders were everywhere, and the newcomers watched the tough webs being woven by the spider from a liquid that it secreted, ready to catch its next meal, or wrap it in a cocoon and save the insect for dinner later.

'I told you it was all doom and gloom down here, didn't I!' said Mr Dozer, matter-of-factly, when the newcomers jumped when something suddenly ran between their legs. And then he whispered to them. 'Now, before we go on our way, I must ask you all to be very quiet as we walk along the tunnels. I am sad to say that, unfortunately, I have bad news.' His face showed a nervous look.

As Pal, Pickle and Patsy followed badger, they noticed wooden props were holding back the earth walls and, at the end of the tunnel they were walking along, the wall was heavily barricaded with more wooden struts. Obviously, no one was meant to go through there.

'Why is that barrier there, Mr Dozer?' asked Pickle, boldly. But he didn't feel quite as bold when he suddenly heard strange noises coming from the direction of the barricade.

Pal looked worried. 'What's that loud noise we can hear? I hope the tunnel won't collapse!'

Without a word in reply, the badger suddenly sat down on a pile of fallen earth nearby and put his head in his paws and sobbed to himself, wiping away his tears with his paw.

His sobbing got Patsy very worried; with concern in her voice, she gently asked the badger, 'Why are you crying? Please don't tell us we are lost!'

Whilst Pal and Pickle were amazed to see the badger, so gruff and stern before, was now reduced to tears. Mr Dozer spluttered as he tried to talk clearly, after wiping his runny nose on his sleeve cuff. 'No... no, you are all quite safe, we are not lost. It's my neighbours who are upsetting me. My life is being ruined by them since they moved in. They have no consideration for me at all.'

He wiped away his tears with a dirty white piece of rag before speaking again. 'I've got moles, you see, that have moved in next door. And if you don't know what a mole is like, I will tell you! They are animals with bad eyesight, and they make the most annoying holes in places you don't want them! If there is anything I dislike—it's moles! They truly are "neighbours from hell"!'

'Why don't you like them, Mr Dozer?' asked Pal, warily, not wanting to upset him further but wanting to know more.

'Why don't I like them! Why don't I like them!' he replied, sneeringly. 'It's because—it's just not fair!'

'What's not fair?' quizzed, Pickle tactfully. He knew all about moles himself, as they had lived in the fields on the farm, and the only trouble they had caused was creating mounds of earth everywhere, as they burrowed below ground.

The badger then looked sternly at the newcomers as he replied, 'Because it was *my* ancestors that showed the tall people the advantages of making tunnels—yes!—by copying the work of badgers!'

'Like what, Mr Dozer?' asked Pal curiously, eager to know more.

'I don't suppose you've heard of coal mines, copper mines or salt mines? Or even tunnels for cars and trains to use. We badgers have played a very important role in history to show others the advantages of building tunnels.' His voice had a bragging tone as he spoke, as he was very proud of his ancestors.

'That's fantastic, I must say Mr Dozer,' said Pickle, respectfully. 'You badgers are very clever and knowl-edgeable as well. I would be very proud indeed to have ancestors that have shown the importance of tunnel-building to the world.' Pickle now had renewed admiration for the sad-looking badger. Although, he really hadn't understood much of what the badger had said, but his friend Pal looked very impressed.

'I think it's fantastic too,' added Pal kindly. 'But it doesn't explain why you dislike moles, especially as they are your neighbours?'

'Well, if you must know,' replied the badger, 'moles are silly furry creatures with beady little eyes, who think *they* know how to build tunnels better than us! Huh! A mole's tunnel is nothing compared to a badgers—especially mine!'

Pal gave the piglets a sideways glance. They were trying not to snort behind their trotters.

The badger huffed, then continued, 'And it's laugh-able to think they push up the earth into mounds as they tunnel, so that the tall people know where they are! Because, you see, even they don't like them because they do so much damage to gardens and fields!'

'But, that still doesn't explain why you sound so angry towards them,' asked Patsy, as sweetly as she could. 'Are you, maybe, jealous of them for some reason?'

Mr Dozer spluttered as he replied, knowing that the little piglet was correct but not wanting to admit it. 'Well, do you think this is fair...? Humans, the tall people, invented a big powerful machine that can burrow into the earth, just like myself. And what did they call this machine, I ask you!? Yes, that's right! A "MOLE"! Yes, they only went and named it after those stupid moles! What about ME? Don't I and all other badgers deserve some recognition?'

The three friends nodded their heads in agreement but really wanted to giggle. Patsy thought to herself, with her answer: *Mr Dozer was indeed a very jealous badger!*

Mr Dozer then got off the pile of earth he had been sitting on and said, abruptly, 'Follow me newcomers!' He then led them towards the end wall where the struts were firmly in place. 'Just listen to them!' he whispered to the three friends, 'Moles, plotting and scheming and obviously up to no good! And that is my tunnel they have broken into, my territory, my home!' The badger then looked at the group of friends to see if he had their full attention as he carried on speaking to them in a low voice. 'They tried to force their way into this part of the tunnel recently. That's why this barricade is here—to keep them out!' He wiped away another tear. 'But come with me and I'll show you where we can see what they are up to now!'

Pal, Patsy and Pickle watched the badger as he opened up a large door in the biggest root in the tunnel. 'Come on now, Pal, you lead the way like before; just slide down inside the root and I can assure you it will be a safe landing.'

Pal did as he was asked. And safe it was, as one by one, they all tumbled down the tree root to another level below.

'I quite enjoyed that!' exclaimed Pickle laughing, as he picked himself up. 'This certainly is like a new world to us, below ground, Mr Dozer.' He hoped that talking kindly to the badger would make him a bit more amiable to be with.

Whilst Pal was deep in thought about how an animal who had spent his whole life underground, apart from coming out night-time, could know so much about the outside world. There was something very strange about this very knowledgeable Mr Dozer.

CHAPTER 10

THE EXTERMINATORS

'Come, follow me!' said the badger, rather abruptly, as he stressed to the three friends to listen to those wretched moles.

Pal, Pickle and Patsy followed closely behind him, but quickened their pace when they saw earth falling from above. Also, they could hear the sound of thumping nearby. When at last they stopped by another tree root, they were amazed when Mr Dozer opened up a door in another root. Inside was a strange tubular structure with slanting mirrors, the likes of which they had never seen before.

'It's a periscope!' said the badger with pride, when he saw the puzzled look on the faces of the newcomers. 'Take a look into it Pal, and you can see what the moles are doing above us. We can spy on them with this!'

'Do you think I should, Mr Dozer?' asked Pal, warily. 'After all they are your neighbours and goodness knows what they might be doing.'

'Neighbours! Neighbours! Baah! You should hear

the noise they make during the day when I'm trying to sleep. Wild parties, I believe. And at night I see them sneaking off in a gang with a strange metal object and carrying sacks. I just know they are up to no good. And now they want my tunnels because they know about my secret!'

Pickle's ears twitched. 'Secret! What's your secret?'

'You'll find out later!' the badger replied with a slight smile.

'Ok, I'll take a look,' agreed Pal, rather reluctantly, especially as he was feeling extremely worried about the noise and the falling earth. He would sooner have been on their way than hanging around to see what was coming, but he took his place in front of the periscope and was soon amazed at what he could see above him. The first thing that he noticed was a gang of four moles, deep in conversation, with one bossy mole ordering the others about. But, unlike the tiny moles on the farm fields, these moles were very large.

And then Pal noticed the strange metal object that the badger had mentioned. Suddenly he realised what it was! He whispered back to the eager waiting group. 'It's a metal detector. I've seen humans use them to search in the fields for treasure. And it looks like they have a sack full of items—probably gold!'

'GOLD!' oinked the piglets, excitedly.

'What's gold, Pickle?' asked Patsy. 'Is it tasty to eat?'

Pal chuckled. 'No—shhh! Let me watch, so I can see just what they are planning.' Everyone was silent as he continued to spy on the moles. 'Oh, dear!' he suddenly gasped, 'We've got trouble, Mr Dozer. They have a wooden battering ram, which they are taking below. It looks like they intend to break into your tunnels.' Pal tried not to sound dramatic, but he felt nervous especially as they were all underground.

'I knew it! I knew it!' snarled Mr Dozer. 'I knew it wouldn't be long before the moles tried their antics again. Come on you three, follow me quickly! We have to get down to the lower tunnels, as that's where they tried to break through last time. And I haven't completed the barricade yet!'

Mr Dozer rushed down a nearby slope and then along another tunnel, moaning as he did so, closely followed by the newcomers. Soon they were all standing in front of an earth wall, secured only by a few wooden beams. Pal realised it wouldn't take much for the invading moles to break that down, after all, the moles were so much bigger than an average mole.

'We want to help you, Mr Dozer,' said Pal in a concerned voice, as he looked at the worried face of the badger. He felt alarmed, because he had noticed that the bossy mole had been wearing a mask over his eyes. And he also knew that the orange and black striped jumper he wore was the colour of danger, like a bee or wasp. Scrumpy, the little moonling man had told him that some snakes were venomous if they were that colour.

'Have you a plan, Mr Dozer?' Pal continued. 'If so, I think you should tell us it quickly!'

Mr Dozer looked a bit forlorn and sorrowful as he replied, 'I can't fight these neighbours anymore, Pal. I think my tunnelling days are over! I am too old for all this worry and hassle.' Then with a look of defeat he gently added, 'If they break through, I want you all to follow me quickly into this emergency lift, which will take us down to safety. Do you all understand?'

The three friends nodded, sadness in their hearts at seeing the badger so distressed. Mr Dozer pulled a lever on the tunnel wall and a door opened in the earth wall, revealing a box-like room, that he explained was the lift.

'I think it is unfair that you are being driven out of your home by these moles, Mr Dozer,' said Pal firmly.

'We could help you fight them,' said Pickle enthusiastically. He was feeling quite upset about seeing the distress on the badger's face.

'Yes, we sure will!' agreed the other two friends.

Mr Dozer looked overwhelmed at the kindness that was being shown to him. And he secretly wished he hadn't been so outspoken to Pal when they had first arrived at his sett. 'I cannot believe that you all are prepared to help me when I haven't actually been very welcoming to you all, which I'm sorry for,' he said. 'But, I am also sorry that we have nothing to fight the intruders with.'

Pal then sounded excitable as he replied quickly. 'But we have! We have these hooded gowns!' He lifted his paws up. 'Do you remember what I said when we first put them on—we look like ghosts! Let's scare the life out of those giant moles!' The animals all nodded at Pal's wise words. 'We must all charge at the intruders as they break through the barricade, and then yell as loud as we can—ghostly sounds! Hopefully we will frighten the life out of them and scare them away. Surely that's better than doing nothing at all!'

'It's worth a try, Pal! Of course it is!' replied the badger. 'Thank you sincerely, all of you, for trying to help this grumpy old badger.' The badger spoke quickly because he knew it wouldn't be too long before the wall gave way and the battle could begin.

Pal then waved his two front paws as he stood up on his hind legs. He knew how to beg like this but hoped he could stay upright for longer this time, without falling over. 'Can you all make these noises, "Wooah! Wooah! Wooah!" as we go forward, and then Mr Dozer, Pickle and myself will shout loudly, "Booooooo!"'

'And Patsy,' interrupted Pickle, 'I want you to stand safely behind us three, just making as much noise as you can!'

'Oi! I will certainly not!' squealed Patsy, annoyed with Pickle being so protective of her. 'I'm standing by your side in the battle!'

Pickle was taken aback and said, 'Sorry, my piggy-wiggy, Patsy...' He felt such love for Patsy and thought she was actually much braver than himself.

Before long, louder sounds came from the other side

of the barricade—the noise of fast-approaching bur-
rowing moles.

'Are we all ready now?' said Pal, seriously. 'Dim the
lanterns, Mr Dozer, and please pull our hoods down
well, over our heads. Good luck everyone! And remember, when I say "Charge!" we all go forward together
making as much noise as we can!'

'And when I shout retreat, you all run to the lift!'
added the badger, who secretly felt they were definitely going to be invaded by the moles very shortly.

The group patiently waited, as the banging became
louder and louder, and the battering ram was thumped
against the weak spot in the earth wall. Before long, a
gaping hole started to appear and the wall and beams
began to collapse.

The moles came into view but were caught off guard,
as they had not expected to see what they now saw
in front of them: Four white, cloaked figures suddenly
rushed towards them, wailing loudly with the sounds
of 'Wooah! Wooah! Wooah!' and 'Booooo!' and other
strange eerie noises. And then a piercing shriek was
heard by the moles, in a ghostly manner, going... 'EX-
TERMINATE!'

Unfortunately, Pickle still had wind from being so

greedy earlier on, and with all the excitement of the attack, gave out the loudest 'raspberry' parp ever!

One of the moles shouted out in despair. 'We've only broken into a ghost compound! They have to be the Ghost Squad Exterminators, who hate us moles and kill us!' All the moles were now choking, and wafting away Pickle's offending stink, as they retreated backwards, because of the ever-louder ghostly howling.

'Quickly, throw that bundle at them!' yelled one of the moles. 'And then run for your life!'

A bulky sack flew through the opening and landed at the feet of the ghosts—with a clunk!

'That's our treasure you've just thrown at them you pesky mole!' came an angry voice through the gap in the wall, followed by the words, 'Run moles, run! Not just from these exterminators, but from ME! The "Mad Mole"—that's if I survive this stink!'

After the scurrying and shouting by the moles, as they fled from the ghostly-looking newcomers, and the, so called 'Mad Mole', a silence fell on the group, as they listened to make sure the moles had fled.

They've gone!' laughed Pal, feeling relieved. 'We've seen them off, Mr Dozer!' But then he noticed the earth all around them was falling faster, and the opening in the earth wall was about to finally collapse completely.

'Quick! Into the lift!' shouted Mr Dozer, who was well aware of the dangers of a collapse inside a tunnel. 'Don't forget to pick up the sack, Pal.'

Once they were all safely inside, Mr Dozer slammed the lift door shut. 'Hold on now; this could be a bumpy ride down. Here we go!'

The lift descended, rapidly, down into the depths, all the while they could hear the sound of falling earth landing on the roof of the lift.

'I feel frightened,' whispered Patsy. 'My tummy is in my mouth!' She moved closer to Pickle but realised his fear was causing his tummy to make wiffy aromas, so she quickly backed away, holding her trotter up to cover her snout.

'Nearly there, Patsy,' said Mr Dozer, as he smiled kindly at her. 'Take deep breaths if you are feeling sick.'

'Is that wise, Mr Dozer,' said Pal with a laugh, as he looked at Pickle.

The lift came to a sudden stand-still with a bump.

'Into here, quickly, all of you!' yelled Mr Dozer, as he pulled a nearby lever, which opened up a large stone door. When they were all through he closed the door and said, 'We are quite safe now. This is a stone chamber, so we can all relax.'

'Thank goodness we scared the moles off!' gasped Pal, who was delighted to hear that they were all safe from danger.

The badger smiled widely, as he looked at his new friends, 'I just want to say to you all how grateful I am for your help. Because, without it, I dread to think what might have happened.' Mr Dozer gazed at each of the newcomers tenderly, as he added, 'Please forgive my abrupt manner to you all earlier. I thank you all for what you have done today.'

'That's alright, Mr Dozer. We were glad to help you,' said Pal, who quite liked seeing a less grumpy badger.

'We certainly made good ghosts!' added Pickle.

Patsy had her say as well, as she said kindly, 'I think we should always help others who are in distress, because, who knows, one day we might need help ourselves!' She looked at the badger and smiled. 'It certainly gives me a warm glow to help a friend in need like you, Mr Dozer.'

'Did you call me... a friend, Patsy?' gasped the badger in an amazed voice at what he had just heard the piglet say.

The three friends nodded, and then they all laughed loudly when they noticed the biggest smile ever spread across the badger's face.

CHAPTER 11

CHAMBER OF MYSTERIES

Everyone gave a deep sigh of relief, as they stood in the dark stone chamber.

'You scared the life out of me Patsy, with your loud exterminate screams. No wonder the moles fled!' said Pal, proudly.

'You were all fantastic,' nodded the badger, who praised them in a far friendlier manner after the terrible events that had just happened.

'What will you do now, Mr Dozer, with all your tunnels being destroyed,' enquired Pickle, with a concerned tone in his voice.

'My days of tunnelling are over now my friends. I shall probably just spend the rest of my days in this chamber and continue to be lonely, as always.' He sighed heavily and shrugged his shoulders. 'But first I owe you all an apology. I am so sorry I was so grumpy towards you all when we first met.'

'It's forgotten,' reassured Patsy. 'But, why are you lonely? Surely you have family and friends.'

'Yes, I do... somewhere. But sadly, all my life, I have been selfish,' Mr dozer replied. 'I had no time for them, or even finding a wife or companion. All I wanted to do was tunnel, and when I wasn't making those, I was stone carving in here—generally alone!'

The three friends felt compassion for the lonely badger.

'No one should spend their life alone, Mr Dozer,' insisted Pal. 'Even badgers need other badgers to talk to, or other kinds of friends. Just look at us three—we are dear friends. Pickle is in love with Patsy—she's his sweetheart'.

Patsy blushed as she glanced at Pickle, who winked back at her.

Pal, smiled and then added, 'And even I hope to find a bride for myself one day.' He thought for a moment. 'I wouldn't want to be lonely and without friends.'

Patsy added, 'And we are *your* friends now.'

'And we like you very much,' said Pickle, kindly.

'But,' said Pal, 'I think we would like you even better, Mr Dozer, if we could have some light in this rather dark place. It's a bit spooky...'

'Of course! Just stand still whilst I light the lanterns on the walls,' the badger replied, a happy tone in his voice after the kindness shown by his new friends. 'And then, before you all go on to the next part of your journey, would you mind if we chatted for a while, because it would be so nice to have company—your company!'

But, the friends didn't have a chance to reply, because the lanterns suddenly cast a warm glow around the stone chamber, revealing a wonderful sight.

'Oh, my goodness!' gasped Patsy.

'Wow, wow, wow!' exclaimed Pickle, lost for a better word.

Pal gazed about at the chamber, wagging his tail. 'This is fantastic, Mr Dozer!' He stared at the strange carvings revealed by the lantern light, and most incredibly, the tomb-like structure in the middle of the room. 'What is it all? It's just amazing! Do tell us about it, please!'

The badger looked coy and yet wore a proud expression on his face, as he went on to explain to the group of friends where he lived. 'This is the work of my ancestors and myself. Every member of my family, throughout the ages has contributed to the carvings on these walls.' He thought for a short while before adding. 'As you are all so interested in this chamber, how about I tell you all about the carvings!' He was delighted to see the newcomers nodding to his suggestion. He paused before speaking again and then added serious-ly, 'I have learned so much myself in this cavern, and it's all thanks to my ancestors, who carved into these walls the exciting adventures they had been on and what interested them.' The badger paused before speaking again; no longer did he sound bad-tempered but spoke in a much nicer way to his new friends.

'And now I must tell you about my grandfather, Hop-along. He is a dear badger who I would have loved you all to meet. Such an interesting character! You three would call *me* a grumpy old badger compared to my interesting grandfather!' He surprised Pal, Pickle and Patsy as he laughed the loudest laugh they had heard from him, which encouraged them to laugh along. They all listened with great interest to what Mr Dozer was saying about his grandfather, who was long departed from this world. But, even so, he smiled widely as he recalled happy memories he fondly had of his relative. 'You three would have liked Grandfather Hop-along,' he said.

'Why was he called "Hop-along"?' asked Pickle.

'Well... because he only had three legs, after an ac-cident! Sadly, he had always wanted to be an explorer but now he could no longer do this. And nothing would make him happy; that was until he was given a large book about a place far, far away, which thrilled him so much, and all he could talk about was this place called Egypt!' As the newcomers listened to every word Mr Dozer was saying, he continued. 'Grandfather was captivated by the history of Egypt and so were we, his grandchildren, me included, as he told us exciting things that he had read about the place. He told us stories of kings and queens that ruled Egypt, long, long ago. These were known as pharaohs and—would you believe it!—when these important people died, they were wrapped in bandages and placed in tombs, very much like the one in my cavern.' Mr Dozer smiled as he looked at the interested faces of Pal, Pickle and Patsy listening with interest. 'And he told us about the band-aged figures, known as "mummies", which were buried in secret places along with lots of treasures.'

Pickle looked at Mr Dozer and said, slightly nervously, 'Wow! That is amazing, Mr Dozer, but I thought all mummies were cuddly and I don't think I would want to cuddle one of those!'

'Don't be silly, Pickle. Not *that* type of mummy!' said Pal gently, 'We must learn all we can from our new friend. Now listen!'

'Ssh, Pal! I want to listen to Mr Dozer,' said Pickle as he gave his friend a cheeky smile.

Patsy, looked worried, 'But, isn't that a tomb in your cavern?' Everybody looked over at the magnificent structure. 'Is there anyone inside it?' she gulped. Pickle trotted behind her, as they all waited for the reply.

'No, no Patsy,' replied Mr Dozer. 'Remember me telling you that my grandfather was excited at what he learnt about Egypt, well, in his time, this tomb was once a large rock, so creating this tomb became the love of his life. And you will notice all around are strange words and pictures, which are all his work. I think you will all agree with me, it is an amazing tribute to Grandfather Hop-along and Egypt.'

'I think it's wonderful, and I can see you are so proud, and rightly so!' said Pal.

Patsy and Pickle both nodded eagerly in agreement.

'Who said you were going to be grumpy, Mr Dozer!' added Pickle, cheekily, 'How wrong they were, Mr Dozer. I think you have to be the most interesting badger I've ever come across!'

As Pal and Patsy nodded in agreement, the badger grinned with delight and then continued to answer all the many questions they each asked him about Egypt and the other engravings. And he felt the happiest he had felt in a long time.

Mr Dozer was still beaming with joy, while he watched his new friends gazing in wonderment at the carvings on the walls and on the tomb.

'Mr Dozer,' asked Patsy, 'Have you any carvings on the walls that are about the Island?'

The badger beamed with pride. 'I certainly have, Patsy.' The badger beckoned them all to follow him. 'Now this odd-looking building is a castle and has quite a history, I'm told, because a king, a long time ago, was imprisoned there.' He then went onto tell the newcomers what being in a prison meant, before continuing with his story. 'And I happen to also know that, even today, they have donkeys at the castle that walk inside a big wooden wheel to bring up water from a deep well.' Mr Dozer sighed deeply. 'Of course, I haven't actually seen many of the things I am telling you about, but my long-departed Uncle Sylus can verify this, as he was quite the explorer on the Island, and had a reputation for popping up everywhere. He loved to mix with other badgers who told him exciting stories and the adventures they had been on as well.'

The wide-eyed friends all agreed that Mr Dozer's tales were very enjoyable and interesting as they hung on to every word that was being said to them.

'But before we go,' said Mr Dozer, 'I must show you another carving of something that is on the Island. Now what do you think this is?' he said with a chuckle.

The piglets and Pal all looked blankly at him, clueless as they had no idea.

'What you are looking at here is wooden stocks, which you can still see today but no longer in use. Well, a long, long time ago, naughty people used to be locked into these stocks as a punishment! And as they couldn't escape while in the stocks, people used to throw rotten vegetables at them for being bad.'

'Punishment!' squealed Pickle with a snort. 'I call that, bliss! I think I would have enjoyed being put in the stocks and pelted with food! Better than always being hungry like we were on the farm.'

'I can tell you those days are over, Pickle,' laughed the badger. 'You will be well looked after in Harmony Haven. Now, you just have time to all have a last wander around my cavern, whilst I rest my weary legs, and if you have any questions I will be delighted to answer them for you.'

He smiled as he watched his new friends exploring the cavern. How could he ever imagine that two piglets and a dog would bring him so much joy and happiness, and also have the good grace to forgive him for his rudeness to them. He felt like jumping for joy; he was no longer a grumpy old badger; he could become a better badger now! Now that he had been told he was interesting and could tell wonderful stories about his ancestors, he promised himself to be friendly from now on—to everyone!

CHAPTER 12

THE SECRET MASTERPIECE

When the badger had rested for a while, Pal called over to him. 'Which ones are your carvings, Mr Dozer?'

Hearing what Pal had asked, the badger once again beckoned to them all to follow him to another part of the chamber. 'This is my work. I would love to tell you about it,' he said proudly, as he pointed to a carving that he had framed by etching around it into the stone, which had made it look like a beautiful picture.

The badger watched the newcomers for a while, aware that they were trying to fathom out what the carving resembled. And then, after a while, he said wisely to them, 'Now listen carefully, whilst I explain to you what you are seeing, but I will only tell you if you each promise to keep it a secret.' He fixed his eyes seriously on the trio of friends.

'We promise!' they all agreed, eager to know Mr Dozer's secret.

The badger nodded and looked at the carving. 'I believe this to be my masterpiece, the best carving I have ever done,' he said proudly, stepping back to admire his work. 'And only the inhabitants of Harmony Haven know about this secret.'

'This sounds really exciting,' said Pal, whose eyes kept glancing over towards the Egyptian writing that was carved into the walls. With each symbol having its own meaning, he was desperate to understand and know more.

The badger then pointed out the meaning of the carving, the eyes of the friends watching him with interest. 'Look at these round circles here, which we can see in the sky. This one here is the moon that comes out at night, and this other round disc is the sun, which comes out during the daytime. And over here is our Earth, that we all live on.'

'But, it shows the Earth being round! I thought the earth was flat!' said Pickle, perfectly seriously.

Patsy chuckled. 'Don't be silly, Pickle!'

'Your lovely partner is correct, Pickle, you are most definitely wrong there! The earth is round and that's been proven by science,' smiled Mr Dozer kindly at the little pig. He would have liked to have explained in more detail, but he knew their time was limited before they had to go on the next part of their journey. 'What I am showing you now are these other planets that are so very far, far away and look so tiny in the carvings. They can only be properly seen with telescopes.'

Patsy prodded a long object with her trotter. 'What's that strange shape, there?'

'That, my dear, is a spaceship; it travelled through the skies, faster than we can imagine. It went from planet to planet with other kinds of beings on board—who, I should say, were very different from ourselves!'

In the chamber there was not a sound, only the voice of the badger, because Pal, Patsy and Pickle were spellbound, as they listened to every word that was being said by this very interesting badger. Mr Dozer's voice then grew excitable, as he stressed that the spaceship had become damaged during the journey and was lost in space, battered and out of touch from its home planet, and the spaceship travelled on and on. And then—a miracle!—those on board spotted a planet in the distance, which turned out to be Earth! Knowing they had to land somewhere, the travellers made the decision to secretly land on our planet.'

'Wow! Wow! Please tell us more, Mr Dozer,' gasped

Pickle, whose eyes, like Patsy's and Pal's, were wide open with excitement.

The badger laughed. 'Look at this diamond-shape carving. It's the Isle of Wight, the Island, our home. And this is where the spaceship landed, and inside—oh, you wouldn't believe it! I cannot tell you because you will find out later...'

'It's a fantastic carving!' praised Patsy.

'Yeah, it's brill!' grunted Pickle, getting in closer to look at it.

Pal studied it closely. He then asked about the group of strange-looking beings that were carved into the wall, next to the spaceship. 'So, who's this weird creature then... sort of looks like—'

'Please don't ask me!' snapped the badger, cutting Pal off mid-sentence. 'I cannot tell you, but you will find out soon enough!' The badger laughed to himself, as he led them away from his masterpiece.

'I think we could spend hours in here with you, Mr Dozer, listening to you explaining about things we could never have imagined,' said Pal brightly, as he hurried along, glancing about the cavern with delight.

Mr Dozer felt thrilled to see their excited faces, and they were even more amazed when he said with a smile,

'It's no good my friends, I have never been able to keep a secret, so I have to tell you! It was Oliver Gruffle in that spaceship—Sshh!'

The three friends told him how amazed they were at hearing all the stories. In fact, they were all finding it hard to believe everything they were hearing.

Mr Dozer then turned to look at Patsy. 'What carving do you like best, my dear?' he asked kindly.

'I enjoyed the ones where the story was about the spaceship and hearing about our Guardian Oliver Gruffle,' she replied sweetly.

'I agree with Patsy, Mr Dozer,' interrupted Pickle. 'But, I can't believe there is a wonderful big coloured cone hat outside a hospital to make poorly people happy! And that Scrumpy wears a small one on his head! It's no wonder Pal was always happy to see his little friend!' He then added dreamily to himself. 'Maybe, I will wear one myself, as I want to make others happy when they look at me.'

Mr Dozer replied with a chuckle. 'A cone hat would suit you Pickle! What a pity you never wore one at Farmer Muggleton's wretched farm; maybe he might have been a happier person if you had!'

His comments caused loud 'Boo!'s from the three

friends, at the mention of the cruel farmer's name. And then they all laughed along with Mr Dozer.

When they could laugh no more, Mr Dozer addressed Pal. 'Tell me, have you got a favourite carving?' He secretly hoped his masterpiece would be all of their favourite carving, because the badger was probably a bit too proud of his own work.

'Ah, my favourite...' replied Pal, 'Let me see... Yes! I agree with the piglets, I loved your masterpiece.'

'You like something else, don't you?' replied the badger. 'Otherwise, why are you continually looking at the carvings around the tomb?'

Pickle suddenly cried out. 'Wooh! Wooh! I'm coming out to scare you, Pal!' he said, laughing. 'I'm a mummy and I'm going to cuddle YOUUUUU!' He made everyone else laugh at his silly remarks.

But Pal just tutted, as he padded towards the tomb in the centre of the cavern. 'I do love all these carvings, Mr Dozer, and it makes me realise what an exciting world we live in.' Pal glanced back at the beaming badger as he added, 'And it's all thanks to you and your ancestors for making these stories for us to enjoy.'

Mr Dozer nodded happily and managed a wide smile.

Pickle added, 'And that's what the Woodland Warden said as well, Mr Dozer. 'Stop, Look and Listen!'

Patsy giggled, turning to Pal. 'I think that if a ghost or a mummy came out of that tomb, you would run and hide, whilst my Pickle would be brave and ask it what it wanted!'

'I don't think so, Patsy,' replied Pal, giving her a low growl, 'I am not a puppy you know! I'm a fully grown-up dog and nothing scares me!' Pal barked proudly at her to make his point.

Pickle oinked along and said, 'With Pal's growl and snarl and me "oinking" loudly, my friend and I would boldly scare any intruder away—wouldn't we, Pal?'

Pal smiled to himself, for he knew that really, dear Pickle would probably just hide behind him.

Mr Dozer was thinking to himself about the scared look on the faces of the three friends when the moles were breaking into his sett and chuckled to himself keeping quiet. He eventually said, 'Well, my friends, it looks to me as if my carving of Oliver Gruffle, arriving in his spaceship is all your favourite. And rightly so, because without him, there would be no Harmony Haven, and none of us would have met and become... firm friends!'

Pal, Pickle and Patsy thought about the badger's words, and what a wonderful place Harmony Haven was turning out to be with all its secrets.

They could hardly wait to meet their guardian and protector... Oliver Gruffle!

CHAPTER 13

UNCLE SYLUS

Suddenly, a knocking sound echoed around the chamber, which became louder and louder with every knock.

'They're back!' exclaimed the three friends in disbelieve.

'Calm down, don't panic! It's not the moles,' laughed Mr Dozer, with a knowing smile. It's only Uncle Sylus.'

'Uncle Sylus! Where is he then?' Pal asked warily, as they all looked towards the tomb, where the knocking sound appeared to be coming from.

Mr Dozer pointed to the sarcophagus. 'He's in the tomb.'

'What, inside?' Pal yelped, as he felt the piglets jostle in to take a look. 'Is-is-he a mummy then?' speaking with a tremble in his voice but tried to act the bravest of them all.

The badger laughed again and said in a matter-of-fact voice. 'No, don't be silly. He's only a ghost. This chamber has always been haunted.' Badger threw up his paws and went 'Whoooah!' as a joke, making the three friends jump with fright, forgetting that only a few minutes ago they had all said how bold they would be if ever they came face-to-face with a real ghost or a mummy.

'Only... a ghost!' they all exclaimed together.

'So, you knew all about ghostly sounds?' said Pal, as he looked at the grinning face of Mr Dozer.

Suddenly an eerie voice howled out from the tomb, 'I'm coming ouuuut!'

'No, you're not!' yelled back Mr Dozer. 'I've got friends here with me!'

'You can't stop meeeee!' came back the reply, just as a wisp of cloudy mist escaped from the corner of the tomb.

The three friends were transfixed as the ghostly badger form of Uncle Sylus floated up and perched himself on top of the tomb. They could see his eerie shape was that of a badger but with a red stain on his chest area, which appeared to go right through his misty outline.

'These are my friends,' boasted Mr Dozer, addressing his uncle.

'Huh! Since when have *you* had friends, Nephew?' Uncle Sylus replied, icily.

Mr Dozer huffed, ignoring his rude uncle. 'Pal, Pickle, Patsy... this is my Uncle Sylus. As you can see, he is a ghost and shouldn't really be in our world with living creatures. Even though he is departed, he likes to be nosy and keep an eye on me. He is not to be feared, but please forgive the way he smells!'

'How rude!' replied the ghost of Uncle Sylus, eyeing Mr Dozer with a spooky gaze.

Patsy and Pickle giggled behind their trotters, but Pal approached, still being wary. 'Hello,' he said, 'I've never met a ghost before.'

The ghost nodded an acknowledgement. 'Well, now you have!'

'With respect, Sylus, what do you want?' questioned Mr Dozer, impatiently. 'Can't you see I am busy?'

'What I want is, to listen to intelligent conversation for once, like I have heard here today,' replied the ghost exuberantly. 'Let's face it, Bull, you are the most grumpy badger that ever lived—always moaning to me how lonely you are! And yet, never prepared to do anything about it!' The ghost glanced at the friends and then continued talking in his rather eerie voice. 'But, today Nephew, I have had a change of heart about you. I actually feel proud of you, for once. So, just carry on talking all of you, as if I wasn't here.'

Mr Dozer looked proud of himself. 'Well, thank you Uncle, I know you have found me difficult, but I do appreciate the fact that it has been you that has kept me company for so long. But, Uncle, I have made new friends here today, who have taken so much interest in the work of our ancestors and myself that I feel I can now be a very different kind of badger.' The badger then looked his ghostly uncle in the eyes, as he said firmly. 'I know my parents asked you to keep an eye on me, once they were gone, but I don't think they meant for you to keep to that promise—once you were dead! You should be with your own kind now.'

Pal, Pickle and Patsy listened with interest to the conversation that was going on. They each wondered why the ghost kept calling Mr Dozer, 'Bull'? *Could it be a nickname?*, they each thought.

'Well, I have something to tell you, Nephew,' said Uncle Sylus, with a grin. 'I have grown tired of haunting this chamber and keeping an eye on you all these years. I too need a life of my own with my own kind, so I am telling you now that I'm leaving!'

'Leaving!' replied Mr Dozer. 'But, where will you go?'

'I am going off haunting somewhere else.'

'But, surely you have been happy in the Hidden Darkness below?

'Yes, I was, until the younger ghosts took up paint-balling!' He spoke indignantly, as he pointed to his chest area, which had the red stain mark. 'Just look at my ghostly shape; see my front, see my back stained with paint from the paintball that passed right through me! What a mess I look!'

The three friends couldn't help but notice Mr Dozer had a slight smile on his face, but why would he be happy about his uncle leaving?

'Don't worry, Bull,' the ghost continued, 'today I feel as if I have come alive again. I heard ghostly sounds calling from the tunnels above in your world. It rather excited me, so I'm going to find these other ghosts and have some fun in my old age.'

Pickle was about to tell him that it was they who had pretended to be ghosts but Mr Dozer quickly said, 'If my Uncle Sylus wants to go, it's fine with me!'

'I must say Nephew, you have certainly taken my de-parture very well,' stated the ghost. 'Now if you don't mind, like I said before, I would just like to sit here and listen to you all chatting before I depart.'

The friends felt less afraid of the ghost now, having been introduced, although they did all feel uncomfortable watching him sat on top of the tomb, picking at the claws on his feet.

The ghost noticed he was being watched and said, 'Just smartening myself up for my departure!' He gave an icy laugh. 'You never know who I might meet. I quite fancy a romantic encounter!'

'Uncle, why don't you realise you're dead,' sighed Mr Dozer. He ushered his friends away and whispered to them. 'Thanks to all of you for keeping quiet about us making the ghost sounds.' He gave a little chuckle. 'I've been wanting him to leave for ages to be honest—can't stand the smell!'

Not wanting to sound rude, Pal whispered back. 'Is it his feet that smell, or his armpits, or maybe even his breath? I mean, I have been known, at times to get... dog breath!' he sniggered.

Mr Dozer laughed at this. 'No Pal, he's just windy! Us badgers eat worms and insects, but I dread to think what he must eat in the Hidden Darkness, which is one of the Outer-Lands of Harmony Haven.'

Seeing Mr Dozer laughing and looking so happy now, filled Pal, Pickle and Patsy with delight and they too joined him in laughing about his remarks about Uncle Sylus.

'Laughter! Do I hear laughter from you, Bull?' interrupted Uncle Sylus, as he emitted a croak, as if he was trying to join in with the laughter as well. 'My word, Nephew! What a good influence your new friends are having on you! I do hope you realise how lucky you are to know them.'

And then, having listened to what the badger ghost had to say, they all started to laugh even louder, but mainly at the horrible croaky sound that was being made by Uncle Sylus as he tried his best to join in and laugh along.

CHAPTER 14

PAL'S BRILLIANT IDEA

Pal was deep in thought as they continued being shown more of the interesting carvings, when he suddenly had an idea. 'Have you ever shown any other animal, or being, this wonderful chamber, Mr Dozer?' he asked excitedly with a broad grin.

The badger shook his head before saying, 'No, it's only been my badger relatives, from time to time and no one else. Why do you ask?'

'I only ask because you have told us that you are a lonely badger and you really cannot spend your old-age feeling this way, because you need to make friends.' Pal noticed Patsy and Pickle were nodding their heads in agreement at his words. 'Just look at what you have explained to us today. I speak for my friends as well, but what a wonderful storyteller you are, as well as being a Grand Master at making tunnels, and a fantastic master stone carver. You, my friend, could be a Master of Teaching, if you would only let others into this chamber to admire your work and the work of your ancestors. I don't think you would be lonely again if you are pre-pared to make friends with others.'

'It's true what Pal is saying, Mr Dozer,' said Patsy eagerly. 'Just look at what you have taught us all here today. We would never have known about so many events if it hadn't been for you.'

Pickle added, 'And you have so much patience with all the questions we have asked. Surely, you must agree with Pal's words.'

Mr Dozer wiped away the tears from his eyes with a grubby piece of rag, before saying, 'You make me feel very humble to hear all of your wise words. He then looked at Pal. 'Can you guide me, Pal, because you cer-tainly are a very wise dog indeed; in fact, the best dog I have ever come across!'

'Oh, you can say that again, Mr Dozer! Pal is not only wise, but highly intelligent and kind!' bragged Pickle proudly enjoying praising his dear friend.

'Anything else, Pickle?' grinned Pal, but he wished Pickle didn't hold him in such high esteem as it made him feel uncomfortable.

'Yep, you are very good-looking—for a dog!' he chuckled.

'Cheeky! Then it's good you have me as your friend,

Pickle,' barked the Border collie. 'Because how many times have you told me that you want to be just like me. I like having you as a friend, as well as Patsy.'

Then the three friends all noticed Mr Dozer was also laughing at their remarks, and they felt delighted at the change in him. Now they were looking at a much nicer and happier badger than the one they had met earlier.

And another one who was delighted was Uncle Sylus, who kept repeating to himself, over and over again, as if he couldn't believe what he had heard, 'My nephew, Bull—a teacher! I'm very impressed and so very, very proud.'

Pal looked around the cavern. 'Mr Dozer, you do not need any guidance from me. You have a wonderful and very interesting room. And you have shown the piglets and I what a fantastic teacher you are. And it is you, my friend, and only *you* that has brought these stories to life again for us.' Pal noticed with delight the elderly badger was listening to every word he was saying. 'So, I suggest to you, throw open the door to this chamber, spread the word—what a wonderful place you have here and let others come and enjoy the work that you and your ancestors have created.'

The badger nodded his heavy head. 'Do you know,

I honestly never thought anyone would be interested in my work, but you all have shown me otherwise.' He beamed with pride, as he dabbed at tears from each eye. And then, to everyone's surprise, he threw his arms around Pal. 'You really are the best dog I have ever come across. Just imagine it! My own Chamber of Mysteries, opened up for everyone to enjoy! It's going to be marvellous, and I will make lots of friends and have happy days ahead!'

'Told you he was clever, Mr Dozer, didn't I!' grinned Pickle, with a proud look on his pink face.

'I want to say thank you to all of you,' said Mr Dozer. 'So, when I open this door, you all must be my first visitors, and we will have a tea party together.'

'It won't be worms, will it, Mr Dozer?' said Patsy, turning up her snout, as she remembered how many the badger had eaten on their way through the tunnels.

The badger laughed as he patted her head. 'No, my dear, I will provide the best food that piglets and dogs love—trust me! I am going to have a lot of work to do first though. Now, I can tell you my secret that those moles were after. My ancestors always brought back any item they found in the earth as they dug. I have drawers here that are full of treasures. I shall put them on display for everyone to see.'

'Wow! Like a... like a...' spluttered Pal, grasping for the word.

'MUSEUM!' shouted Pickle, as all eyes fell on him.

'Yes, Pickle! A museum! Goodness me! What a wise group of friends I have!' praised Mr Dozer in an astounded voice.

Pal watched Pickle cockily strutting around the chamber, quite surprised at the piglet's knowledge. 'How did you know that?' he asked.

Pickle beamed. 'I was having one of my wise moments!'

But the truth was, Pickle had no idea how he knew that word; it had just popped into his mind—like magic!

Suddenly the spooky voice of Uncle Sylus was heard. 'As head of this family, I should have my say, Bull!'

'Which is?' asked Pickle, still feeling very proud of himself, but he also felt Pal had done far more than his share of talking—but he also wanted to show Patsy he was not afraid of a ghost!

All eyes were on the ghost as he said, 'I like the idea of a Chamber of Mysteries and having a party as well for us, but I think we should also include ghost walks. Young animals and other beings love to be scared! Whooooah!'

'Ghost walks!' queried the three friends, who wondered what that was all about.

'But, Uncle, you are going away, remember? So, what's the "us" bit?' asked Mr Dozer impatiently, secretly wishing his Uncle would just go. 'Besides, have you forgotten, Uncle... you are... well—DEAD! Or had you forgotten being squashed by that tractor!'

'Oh, yes... thanks very much for reminding me of my tragic ending!' he replied sarcastically. 'But, I really wouldn't mind showing your friends what it is like in the Hidden Darkness where I live. With all the skeletal bodies of spiders and creepy things around, and of course badger ghosts, I think it would be very thrilling for them down there!'

'No, they wouldn't!' said Mr Dozer, sternly, but he was thinking to himself that, perhaps, a haunted house would be exciting, but maybe not down in the Hidden Darkness! He then saw the puzzled look on the faces of the newcomers, so he went on to explain to them what a ghost walk would be like, with ghosts popping out to scare visitors. 'But then, I suppose this place is haunted with Uncle Sylus, who always keeps appearing.'

The badger looked to the tomb, where his uncle had been sitting only moments before. 'Oh? He's gone! At last!'

But he spoke too soon as an eerie voice came from the tomb, 'Don't fret Nephew, I'm just spraying myself with my skunk spray! I have decided that now you will not be lonely again, I can leave you to your own life. I am off on an exciting adventure with some new ghosts I heard earlier.'

Mr Dozer beamed with happiness. 'Well, my friends, what a day this has been; not just for you all starting your new life, but for me as well, and I can confess, when Oliver Gruffle asked me to be your second guide, I nearly refused but, as you can see by the smile on my face, I am so happy I agreed. Meeting you all has changed my life for the better!'

CHAPTER 15

RUPTIONS AND ROMANCE

Patsy peered into the sack, which the mole had thrown at them in their battle earlier. She was enthralled when she had spotted something shiny inside. 'Do you think we could see what is in here?' she asked Mr Dozer, curious in anticipation.

'I don't see why not,' he replied gently, as he came over to investigate. 'It will be interesting to see what is in there.'

The three friends gasped, as the badger gently emptied the contents of the sack onto the floor of the chamber. Some of the items shone as bright as gold, whilst others were caked in mud. The friends gazed at the treasures encrusted with precious stones and jewels.

'So, this is treasure!' said Pickle, rooting around in the bag with his snout. 'Where do you think the moles got all this from, Pal?'

Pal looked at Mr Dozer for confirmation. 'I believe I am correct in saying that the mole mobsters used that metal detector to find these precious items in fields on the Island. Do you agree, Mr Dozer?'

'I concur, Pal!' replied the badger. 'You see, Pickle and Patsy, you've heard me tell you today about the people who were called Romans, and how they lived on our Island for hundreds of years. Well, looking at these items here, which are Roman coins, I believe this hoard is Roman treasure.'

'I would love to know, why they buried it?' said Pal, excitedly. 'Maybe they thought it would be safe whilst they were out fighting in battles.'

'I know Oliver Gruffle will know exactly what to do with this treasure,' said Mr Dozer. 'It is no use to us in Harmony Haven'.

'What are all these lovely things?' asked Patsy, who was bewitched at seeing the glittering items.

Mr Dozer picked up brooches, crowns, ornaments, coat clasps and many coins. And where he could, he explained what the items were used for. He also showed her the precious stones—rubies, diamonds and sapphires, which the little piglet got very excited about. Patsy then picked up a gold ring, heavily encrusted in coloured jewels, which she thought was really beautiful. 'Do you know what this is for, Pal?' she asked the wise dog, as she placed the ring back on the ground.

Pal studied the item before explaining its purpose to her. 'Ah, now, this is called, a ring! A human boy would hold it in his hand and say to the girl he loved, something like "With this ring, I marry you", and he would place it on her finger. But, in your case, Patsy, if I was that boy, I would have to slip it on your tail like this...' Pal admired the golden ring as he placed it on her tail with his mouth. 'Now we are wed!' he joked.

Silence echoed around the chamber.

'What!' Pickle squealed, wildly, oinking in alarm. 'How could you, Pal! Patsy is my girl! How could you marry her!'

'Don't be silly, Pickle, no I haven't!' insisted Pal, and a bit stunned at his friend's outburst.

'I don't want to be married to Pal,' screamed out Patsy in dismay.

'I'm NOT married to you, Patsy!' replied Pal, trying to calm her down with puppy-dog eyes. 'You're not my type anyway!'

'What's wrong with my Patsy!?' oinked Pickle. 'She's very beautiful!'

'Yes!' agreed Patsy, matter-of-factly.

Pal was getting himself deeper and deeper in trouble every time he opened his mouth. And Pickle was now furious with his friend.

'I just meant, that she's not a dog!' insisted Pal. 'We are a different type of animal, a different species. And a dog and pig getting married is, well... Can you imagine what our children would look like? A puppy with trotters and a curly tail, who grunted instead of barking! Or a piglet with long hair and a bushy tail, that barked instead of grunting!'

Pal started to laugh at his own comments, but he laughed alone, apart from Mr Dozer, who was smiling to himself in an amused way, whilst Pickle continued to look distraught. Patsy sobbed, unable to believe that Pal had been acting the part, just to show her what the human ring was used for.

All the while Mr Dozer listened to all that was going on. He chuckled to himself at the situation, but he could see his help was needed to quickly restore order. It was the least he could do after they had been so kind and helped him defeat the moles, and he didn't want their friendship to break down.

Suddenly, he had an idea. He would take a chance, because the piglets wouldn't know he was talking a load of rubbish. And anything was worth a try to make Patsy and Pickle happy once more.

'Excuse me, if I could just have your attention for a minute,' Mr Dozer said, seriously. 'I believe I know how to resolve this problem!' He tried his best to sound as if he knew what he was talking about. 'Pal, will you come and help me find another ring please.'

Pal, eager to help, followed the badger to one of the walls and watched as he opened a drawer that was situated below the carvings. Pal gasped as he saw what was inside, because it was filled with objects that, Mr Dozer informed him, had been gathered out of the earth by his ancestors as they dug their tunnels. 'We haven't got time for you to look through all this; just help me quickly to find a ring—the largest size you can!'

Pal used his nose to move items out of the way, until he found the ideal thing. 'Will this do?' He picked up a gold ring with an emblem he didn't recognise.

'Perfect! An Egyptian ring. This will do fine,' replied Mr Dozer, as he gave the sheepdog a wink. Pal was then suddenly aware that something was going on and that the badger had a plan.

Turning towards Pickle, Mr Dozer said, 'We need to get this ring on you, Pickle, and then I am happy to say it will be you that is Patsy's husband, and not your friend, Pal. Would you like me to proceed with the wedding ceremony? The quicker it's done, the better!'

'We would! We certainly would, thank you,' gasped Pickle, who gave a weak smile to the badger and the blackest of looks to Pal.

'Good, then follow me, Patsy and Pickle.' Mr Dozer led them across to columns of stone, asking them to stand between the two columns, which they noticed were adorned with floral carvings. He pointed out two stone blue birds above and the floral displays either side. 'Now, this is what I call a romantic setting for a wedding!'

The two piglets beamed with happiness, as they liked what they saw and were eager to be married.

'You look beautiful,' whispered Mr Dozer to Patsy, as he gently placed a small golden crown onto her head, from the sack of treasure, much to the delight of the couple.

'Thank you, Mr Dozer. I feel like a queen now,' said Patsy, coyly, fluttering her long eyelashes. She gave Pal a smug glare. 'I bet you're sorry that you are never going to have me as your wife!' She turned to look adoringly at Pickle.

'If you are both ready we will begin,' said Mr Dozer. 'Now, Patsy please say these words after me and look at Pickle as you say them, as you are telling him how you feel about him.' Speaking slowly, he said, 'My dear, Pickle, I want to marry you, and I will always be true, so please, my loving piglet—just say, I do!'

Pickle was overcome with emotion at the words she had just repeated after Mr Dozer. But eventually he managed to say, 'I do! I do! Oh, Patsy, my sweet pig-gy-wiggy, those sweet words, I will remember all my life.'

Pal tried to look remorseful, as he said to the badger. 'After those wonderful words, I feel I should make amends to my dear friends, so I also have some words that Pickle can say to his beloved.' Pal smiled at his friend, then added, 'Is that alright with you, Pickle?'

'Certainly,' beamed the piglet in a forgiving tone of voice.

Mr Dozer nodded. 'Yes, I think that would be a good way for you to make amends, Pal, and then after your loving words I will put this golden ring on Pickle's tail, and we will have two very happy married pigs!'

Pal looked at his friend and tried to look sincere, as he hid a weak smile. 'Just say these lovely words to your bride, Pickle. I'm sure she will appreciate what you say,' he said in as humble a voice as he could muster.

Pickle couldn't help but notice that Pal was wearing a slight grin on his face, but he thought maybe Pal felt sorry for what he had done and was trying his best to put on a brave face, knowing that Patsy didn't want to be the bride of a dog. And, besides, all friends fall out with each other, now and then.

Pal began his words. 'Repeat after me, Pickle, these sweet words to your bride: I love you, Patsy, with all my heart—'

The piglet grinned, as he liked what he was hearing, and it made him look tenderly at Patsy as he repeated what Pal had said, 'I love you Patsy, with all my heart—'

Pal couldn't hold out any longer; he burst out, howling with laughter, as he tried his best to keep it together and speak the rest of the words, 'I promise... I promise not to snore and never to parp!'

Pickle and Patsy's jaws were open in shock. Silence fell on the group, apart from a giggling Pal, wagging his tail and spinning in circles of hysteria.

'How could you, Pal!' oinked Patsy. 'Those words are awful! Thank goodness I am not married to such an uncouth animal as you!'

But Pickle then started laughing, and in the end so did Patsy. So much so, it started off Mr Dozer laughing as well. He was laughing so much that he had difficulty pushing the ring onto Pickle's tail.

'Congratulations to you both!' the badger said. 'You are now married! And I wish you both a happy life together.'

Pal was still laughing as he added his best wishes to the happy couple. 'Good luck my dear friends. I am sure the three of us will be very happy in this marriage—ha-ha!'

Mr Dozer pointed above Patsy and Pickle, at the two little blue stone birds that had suddenly come alive and were flying above them, singing the sweetest of songs. And rose petals were falling from the columns, changing from stone into soft pink rose petals and landing around the trotters of the newly-wed couple.

'Oh!' gasped Patsy, in a delighted tone. 'This has been a lovely wedding for us, Mr Dozer and so very romantic. Who did this for us?'

'Me!' interrupted Pal. 'Oh, it was just something I arranged for my two best friends,' he boasted, enjoying their happy faces.

Mr Dozer grinned at Pal as he whispered. 'No, Pal. I think this is the work of Oliver Gruffle!'

CHAPTER 16

THE FAMOUS MR DOZER

It was painful for Mr Dozer to admit, but he knew his kind new friends must finally leave his charge and go onwards to the next part of their journey, but he knew he would sorely miss them as he had so enjoyed their company. He said his farewells and led them through the chamber.

'Pal, could you carry that treasure please and give it to Oliver Gruffle when you meet him,' Mr Dozer said. 'He will know exactly what to do with it!'

Patsy had been looking around the chamber and suddenly announced, 'I don't see a door, Mr Dozer! Are we trapped?'

The badger laughed. 'No, never fear, follow me!' he replied as he led them towards the two engraved columns where the piglets had been married. They watched as he reached up and pressed the centre of a stone flower above the arch, and they all gasped as a large stone door opened up slowly in front of them, revealing a vast cavern beyond.

'This is the door to your future happiness,' said Mr Dozer, somewhat sadly.

'This is also the door to your new future as well!' said Pal. 'And Pickle and Patsy, I'm sure, will join me in saying that you are just amazing. It's been a truly wonderful experience being with you.'

The piglets nodded in agreement and followed the badger through the exit. And then the friends pointed in delight, because they noticed two stone badger statues either side of the doorway, as if guarding the chamber.

Pal turned to badger. 'I know you will make a success of your new venture, and we promise to visit you again.'

'I'd like that very much,' replied Mr Dozer. 'You know my Uncle Sylus was right: I will, in future, always treat other animals and beings just how I would like to be treated, because even I have learnt an important lesson today. I thank you dear friends!'

'Mr Dozer, it's not only you that has learnt a lesson today,' said Patsy sweetly. 'We took another's word that you were "grumpy", but you have been far from that; you have been the most interesting badger we have ever come across!'

'Truthfully?' replied the badger with a wide grin on his face.

'Absolutely!' agreed the three friends.

'I feel touched by all your kind words,' Badger said, his eyes moist. 'I must confess, I have always been a shy animal, which badgers tend to be, but the confidence I have now is all thanks to you three.'

They were just about to leave when Pal suddenly remembered something he'd been dying to ask Mr Dozer. 'Why did your Uncle Sylus refer to you as "Bull"? It's a strange name for a badger—more suited to cattle on a farm!'

'Ah! That's actually my real name, Pal' replied Mr Dozer, with a chuckle. 'Mr Bull Dozer!'

The three friends took a moment to get the joke and then all cackled away.

'And what is so funny about that?' replied Mr Dozer, looking hurt.

'Oh, Mr Dozer,' laughed Pal as he tried not to laugh again. 'Don't you realise that you have been given a huge honour by humans and you don't even realise it, do you?'

The badger looked even more puzzled as he shook

his head, 'Me?' he exclaimed. 'What do you mean? Please, explain!'

'We used to see a powerful machine carrying out work on the farm where we lived,' explained Pal. 'It was used to clear earth out of the way. The humans called it a... "bulldozer"!'

When Pal's revelation had sunk in, Mr Dozer replied, 'My goodness! You mean to tell me that my badger digging ability has been recognised by the tall people up above?! I'm famous! You've made my day.' Mr Dozer gasped and did a little happy dance. 'Now, I bid you farewell... I'm off to find my Uncle Sylus before he leaves for good and maybe I'll get him to teach me how to play a game of paintballing!'

'But I thought your uncle lives in the Hidden Darkness, an Outer-Land of Harmony Haven?' asked Pal, a bit puzzled.

'True, but life is for living, you've taught me that. Besides I've never been into the Hidden Darkness to see where Uncle Sylus haunts—it should be a lark!' said Mr Dozer with a wide happy smile. 'Now, it is time for you to leave me and go on the final part of your journey! If you look over there,' he said, pointing, 'there's someone you know waiting for you, just next to that barrier.'

The badger was still laughing to himself as he disappeared back inside his Chamber of Mysteries. 'Goodbye, my dear friends. I will keep in touch! Oh, and by the way, I must give you a bit of advice for when you meet Oliver Gruffle—never mention the word "MAGIC"!'

'That's what the Woodland Warden said to us also?' said Patsy.

'Yeah,' added Pickle.

There was a silence and then Mr Dozer popped his head back through the doorway and shouted, 'What, that "grumpy", Woodland Warden!!!' And then he bellowed with laughter, shaking his head and shuffling away.

The friends marched on towards the barrier and before long they realised that the badger was right—there was somebody there to meet them that Pal knew, very well...

CHAPTER 17

THE HOVER-ROCKET PLANE

'SCRUMPY!' yelled Pal, the echo bouncing around the cavern. 'Follow me piglets, come and meet your new friend,' the dog said excitedly, as he ran ahead eager to see the little moonling man who had made this journey possible for them all.

'SCRUMPY!' oinked the piglets, excitedly as they enjoyed the sound of their own echoing. They too were eager to meet him after hearing so much about him from Pal.

'Hello, Pal. I'm delighted to see you all made it safely,' replied Scrumpy. He smiled at the little piglets. 'And this must be Pickle and Patsy—a pair of very fine-looking piglets I must say! I am very pleased to see you all got away from that awful farm.'

The two piglets looked wide-eyed at the moon-shaped face of the little man. He was just as Pal had described him.

'Hello, Scrumpy! Thank you for telling Pal how we could reach Harmony Haven. We've had some wonderful experiences on our journey here,' said Pickle brightly, who was having a job not staring at the colourful cone hat the little man was wearing.

'I do love your outfit, Scrumpy,' gasped Patsy, feeling a bit overwhelmed, as she too looked him up and down. 'Yes, we are all very grateful to you.'

Scrumpy smiled at them all. 'Thank you! I was only too glad to help you all. Pal has become a good friend to me, and I couldn't bear to hear how you were all suffering. And I'm glad you have enjoyed your journey so far. But I'm afraid we do have a little bit further to go yet and then you will reach, what we call, the "Home-Land" of Harmony Haven, which is where the animals, myself and some beings all live. And I know you are all going to love it there, as well as your guardian, Oliver Gruffle!'

'We can't wait to meet him, Scrumpy,' said Pal in an amazed voice. 'We have learnt so much today. I can't wait to tell you all about it. You'll never believe what we have to tell you!'

Scrumpy gave a squeaky chuckle as he thought to himself—*Oh yes, I would! Well, I've got another amazing event for you to see. Oliver has arranged for you to see something very exciting!*

The little man then lead the excited newcomers deeper into the cavern, towards a portal, which looked like a barrier with a transparent doorway. He grinned as he heard their gasps when they looked into the abyss, far, far below them. 'Now we are all going to do a bit of plane-spotting,' he laughed gleefully. 'But, first I think I should explain to Patsy and Pickle what a "plane" is as they look a bit confused—bless them!'

The piglets listened with interest to what Scrumpy had to say, but Pal knew all about planes, because he asked wisely, 'How are we going to see planes down here? Aren't they usually found flying, in the sky, not underground!'

Scrumpy looked amused by his friend's confusion. 'Ah, but this plane is called a hover-rocket plane, and it will fly in and out of those tunnels down below. Can you see them?' he enquired as he pointed down. The eager trio all peered down. Pickle felt a bit dizzy.

'Now you mustn't feel afraid as the hover-rocket plane approaches, because it will make quite a noise. Oliver wanted you all to see it in close-up, so he has arranged for it to slowly rise up towards us. And, who knows, maybe one day, you too will want to travel on it! Believe me, it's a very exciting experience!'

Pal answered him bravely, 'We won't be scared, Scrumpy. It'll be nothing after being in the company of ghosts earlier today.'

'That's good to hear,' said Scrumpy. 'And, I believe you not only met a ghost, but a very grumpy badger as well.'

'Actually, Mr Dozer turned out to be a very interesting animal indeed,' said Pickle, matter-of-factly. 'He just needed company and to share his knowledge with others instead of just having a ghost for company.'

'And we are going to see him again soon,' added Patsy, sweetly. 'And he will never be lonely again, because Pal gave him the idea to open his wonderful Chamber of Mysteries for all to see.'

'Well, that's splendid news. I'll have to pay a visit there myself!' said Scrumpy, thoughtfully. 'And I stand corrected for misjudging Mr Dozer. I'm glad to see you are all a caring group of friends. I shall enjoy having the privilege of guiding and looking after you all in your first week in Harmony Haven.'

Suddenly they all heard a humming sound, which startled the friends. It echoed all around, as they tried to detect where the hum was coming from; whatever it was, it was big!

'What is that?' said Pickle, nervously.

'Sounds like a giant bumble bee!' Patsy added, peering into the deep cavern.

'I'd be the first to run if it was,' chuckled Scrumpy. 'Just keep your eyes looking down and you will see what it is. There's no reason to be afraid.'

Just as he finished speaking, a red beam of light began to shine through the darkness of one of the tunnels. It got brighter and brighter, as something came nearer and louder towards them. The two piglets hid behind Pal, while Scrumpy reassured them once again. And then the three friends all gasped together in one voice at their first sighting of the hover-rocket plane.

Slowly it came into view. The newcomers watched in silence at the sleek, shiny red cylinder-shaped plane. Their eyes widened in amazement at what they were seeing. The hover-rocket plane then slowly began to rise up, closer to them, just as Scrumpy had explained it would. Eventually, they were all able to see inside quite clearly.

Scrumpy then pointed out to them, a driver's cabin, the passenger compartment and another area for storage. 'Look!' he said cheerfully, 'The animals inside are all waving at you. See the enjoyment on their faces. None of them look afraid, do they?'

Pal lifted one of his paws and waved back to the watching passengers. He then exclaimed loudly to the piglets, 'Look, you two! There's cats, dogs, and lot of other animals on board! Let's all bark a "hello" to them!'

Eagerly, the piglets waved and squealed—because they couldn't bark—along with Pal's barking, much to the amusement of Scrumpy.

'They're all wearing clothes,' gasped Patsy, in delight, as she tried to see what each of the animals had on because clothes were quite a novelty to her.

Scrumpy gave a sigh of relief as he watched the two piglets edge nearer to the barrier, and then lifted a trotter to wave back at the animals on the hover-rocket plane. He thought to himself that this looked like the first time any of the newcomers had ever used a paw or a trotter to wave at others. He chuckled at the piglets, looking a bit unbalanced on three legs as they waved.

Slowly, the plane began to descend, and the pilot dimmed the lights, as the three friends strained to watch all that was happening.

Pointing to the front of the plane, Scrumpy explained knowingly, 'Just look how bright that beam is in the front of the plane. Do you see, it's being directed down the tunnel that it is about to enter. It's fantastic really, as that beam detects that everywhere is clear and safe for the hover-rocket plane to go on its way.'

'It's terrific!' agreed the piglets, as they watched every movement that was happening below.

'Now don't get a fright, because here comes the warning echo,' said Scrumpy, covering his ears, just as the sound of "Ooot! Ooot! Ooot!" echoed throughout the cavern. 'What do you think of that?' he said, as the plane disappeared out of sight.

'Great!' agreed Pal and Pickle together, although Patsy admitted it scared her just a little, but maybe next time she heard it, she might enjoy it more. After all she had only been used to seeing and hearing tractors and lorries at the farmyard, and now and then, a passing plane or helicopter.

'Maybe one day you will all enjoy travelling on it as well,' said Scrumpy. He couldn't help but notice the delight on the faces of Pal and Pickle.

'I know I would like that,' said Pal, wagging his tail.

'Me too!' agreed Pickle, hoping his bravery would impress his new wife, Patsy. 'Wow! How exciting everything is here!'

Scrumpy smiled to himself as he watched the new-comers peering down into the deep cavern. He thought to himself, how happy he was that they had all made this such a special journey. As the word *journey* came into his mind, he realised they should be on their way again, because the autumn days were getting shorter, sunset arriving sooner.

'Well my friends, what do you think of Harmony Haven so far?' he asked, with a twinkle in his eye.

Patsy looked at the little man and answered quickly, 'I think it's wonderful! And I never thought that, today, Pickle and I would get married! Look, Scrumpy, we've even got rings on our tails to prove it!' Patsy, proudly swung her bottom around for him to see her tail.

Scrumpy smiled and wished them well for a very happy married life together. And then he added, 'I must say not many animals or beings get to wear priceless gold rings. Where did these come from?'

Pal then went on to explain that Mr Dozer had given Pickle his ring, but Patsy's had come from the sack of treasure. He excitedly regaled the battle with the moles and the metal detector, and how Mr Dozer had asked him to give the sack to Oliver Gruffle, because it was no good to Harmony Haven.

'What an interesting time you all have had!' laughed Scrumpy, as he looked inside the sack Pal was holding. 'Oh, my goodness! The tall people on the Island will be thrilled by all this!'

'What will happen to the moles when they are caught, Scrumpy?' asked Pal, curiously.

'Oliver Gruffle will be very upset that the moles have committed a crime and bullied Mr Dozer,' replied Scrumpy. 'They probably will be sent to the School for Standards, to study good manners and behaviour guidance. And when they have completed the course, some retribution will be given by them from Mr Dozer, for all the trouble and unhappiness they have caused him.'

Pickle looked serious. 'What if the moles refuse or continue to cause trouble? What then?"

'My answer is very simple, Pickle—eviction!' replied Scrumpy, sternly. 'Oliver will not allow them to live in Harmony Haven, spoiling the lives of others. They will be returned to somewhere on the Island.' He gave a chuckle and added, 'So, my dear friends, you must all try to behave yourselves here! But, remember, Oliver doesn't mind mischief at all! However, serious crimes are not allowed, as it would be horrible to feel unsafe in your own home and area.'

'I like the thought of a safe place to live,' said Patsy.

'Us too!' squealed Pickle, and Pal barked his approval, remembering the unhappy times at the farmyard.

Then Pal looked quizzically at Scrumpy and grinned. 'Thank goodness Oliver doesn't mind mischief, because I know a mischief-maker who is standing right in front of me!'

'Whatever do you mean?' replied Scrumpy, trying to look innocent. 'Surely, you cannot mean, me?'

'Yes, I do!' called back Pal with an excited yap. 'I believe the Woodland Warden wants a few words with you!'

The little man burst into a loud chuckle and winked at them, which made them know he was the cause of the woodland growing towards them, instead of backwards, just as the Woodland Warden had suspected.

When the laughing calmed down, Pickle added, 'Scrumpy, we've been given a bit of advice from Mr Dozer, and the Woodland Warden. To never mention the word "MAGIC" to Oliver Gruffle! Why?'

'It's strange they should both say the same,' said Pal, curiously.

'And, guess what we saw in Mr Dozer's Chamber of Mysteries!' quizzed Patsy, smiling sweetly at the little man, who she liked very much. 'Mr Dozer gave us a beautiful wedding! And we were amazed to see stone birds and flowers become real flying birds. And the flowers dropped their pretty petals around our feet as well!'

The little man pointed above Patsy. 'Like those!' he said, laughing, as once again he watched the surprised but delighted faces on the newcomers.

'Now, that's got to be magic!' laughed Pal as he tracked the two little blue birds flying above them, tweeting happily round and round. Scrumpy began chuckling with delight, which made Pal think the little man was up to mischief. 'Are you up to something, Scrumpy?'

'Me? No!' chuckled Scrumpy. 'But your protector and guardian, Oliver Gruffle, is! Just take a look over there, at the cavern wall. Oliver wanted you all to see what your future home of Harmony Haven will be like—see the picture! And to think... you will soon be there!'

With bulging eyes, Pal, Pickle and Patsy gazed at the moving picture now displayed on the cavern wall. They gasped in wonder and delight when they saw a beautiful countryside with wild flowers, trees, little hills and streams, and small, round colourful buildings that Scrumpy explained were houses.

'Now, meet your future friends,' said Scrumpy, smiling.

Into the scene came cats, dogs, pigs, hamsters and other types of animals. Many were walking on their hind legs, and some were dressed in clothes, and all chatting happily to each other. And there were animals that were just as they wanted to be, which Scrumpy explained were known as 'free-spirits'.

'It's wonderful, Scrumpy,' giggled Patsy, as her eyes filled up with tears. And for once, Pickle and Pal, although delighting in all they were seeing, were lost for words.

'Oh, look Scrumpy! There's little people there as well! They look just like you!' said Patsy, feeling overjoyed. 'And they're wearing cone hats and clothes just like you, Scrumpy!'

Pal suddenly found his voice. 'Scrumpy, how can we ever thank you for bringing us to this wonderful secret place! I am so overjoyed.'

'I don't need thanks, Pal. If you are happy then I am too!' said the moonling with a wide smile on his round cheerful face. He then added seriously, 'Look! Keep your eyes on the picture, as I would hate you all to miss the ending...'

Pal, Pickle and Patsy eagerly watched what was happening. They laughed as they watched all the animals and little moonlings call to them, 'Welcome to Harmony Haven newcomers!' And then the animals on the screen all surrounded a taller figure that appeared who had a kind, bear-like face and wearing a red suit and a magnificent necklace. Scrumpy continued to chuckle as he watched the three animals staring in amazement at the screen.

Scrumpy then said, 'And that is your guardian and protector... Oliver Gruffle! Notice how our community love him and you will too!'

Pickle was pounding his trotters into the ground with excitement. 'Wow! Wow! Wow! This has got to be MAGIC!'

'Shhhh! Pickle!' squealed Patsy, giving him a nudge. 'Have you forgotten? You are not supposed to say THAT word to Oliver!'

Scrumpy chuckled. 'Then maybe you should all watch the screen and see what happens when you do, because Oliver is starting to have a "Magical Moment", which happens when he hears that word!'

To their amazement, Oliver began to twinkle, his tiny furry ears flashing in gold and silver, and then his whole body twinkled in amazing bursts of starlight too. And every creature and being near to him clapped wildly with delight at what was happening. Then the red-suited figure of Oliver began waving to the newcomers and Pal, Patsy and Pickle all waved back. And then, suddenly, the image disappeared, leaving each of the friends feeling very emotional.

Naturally, it was Pickle who spoke first, bursting with pride at what he had caused Oliver to do. 'Woo! I can't wait to say the word "MAGIC" again and give Oliver another "Magical Moment"! Wasn't it terrific!'

The piglet looked bewildered as Scrumpy was shaking his head. 'As you can see, everyone loves it when Oliver twinkles! Just think what would happen if every time anyone saw him, they said *that* word! Poor Oliver would be twinkling all day! So, be careful, Pickle, because if you do it too much he'll have a bit of fun with the culprit!' Scrumpy chuckled after speaking.

'Have you ever been caught out, Scrumpy?' asked Pal.

'Well... maybe!' replied Scrumpy, rather reluctantly. 'I confess, I have ended up with elephant ears and with a green body! But, the effect didn't last long. But one of the funniest things was seeing one of the foxes, who was always at boasting how brave he was, ended up walking around in pink fluffy slippers after saying the word too much in front of Oliver! But at least Oliver's antics do give us a laugh, but you have been warned!'

Pickle grunted. 'I've changed my mind! Thanks for the warning, Scrumpy!'

'I have never laughed so much in my life,' said Patsy. 'We are all going to be so happy from now on, aren't we!'

Pal and Pickle nodded their heads, as Scrumpy replied, 'You certainly are! That's for sure, my friends!'

CHAPTER 18

THE MISCHIEF MAKERS

'Scrumpy!' barked Pal, suddenly. 'I think I know what Oliver is! I've seen a smaller being, that looked just like him!'

'Really, Pal' replied Scrumpy, raising an eyebrow. 'Well, considering Oliver is the only one of his kind on Earth, that is pretty amazing. Do enlighten us!'

'He's a teddy bear!' said Pal, his tail wagging. 'I have seen quite a few bears being held by children who visited the farm, although those teddy bears were much smaller of course!' But as Pal spoke, Pickle and Patsy just had a blank look on their faces, because they didn't know what a teddy bear was.

'I can see why you think Oliver is a teddy bear, with his bear-like face and tiny ears,' replied Scrumpy, most amused. 'But did you notice that he has real hands, just like mine, and his feet are the same! That's why he wears shoes! And, of course, Oliver talks, but can also laugh!' Scrumpy gave another of his cheerful chuckles that was so delightful to hear before saying, 'Oliver is definitely not a teddy bear, though! No matter how cuddly he looks! Oliver is actually... an alien being who came from another world far, far away!'

Pal, Pickle and Patsy all were open-mouthed, speechless, in astonishment. And not one of them revealed that Mr Dozer had already told them about Oliver Gruffle!

'You mean, Oliver Gruffle is from another planet?' said Pal, his tail wagging.

'Woh!' squealed Pickle.

'What a story! And what a secret!' said Patsy.

'Yes, I know!' said Scrumpy. 'He arrived on the spaceship I was telling you about, all those years ago on the Island. Our wonderful friend is a species of Gruffle, a creature who laughs a lot. And, I can tell you, when he laughs, it sounds like this...' Scrumpy then tried to make a 'gruff-gruff!' noise as he laughed. 'But when he talks he sounds just like a young boy.'

The three friends laughed, amazed at all they were hearing, and at Scrumpy trying his best to mimic Oliver's unique laugh.

Scrumpy then said, 'I want you all to know that Oliver and myself have been best friends for a long, long time. And he is a wonderful, kind being, who is loved by everyone and will be a good friend to you all as well. But, we must keep Oliver a secret, because he has unbelievable alien special powers, as you have already seen. However, he uses this power for all of the community, to benefit us all. So, my friends, you all are in for a wonderful new life with Oliver Gruffle, who will never let you down, always take care of you and love you...'

'Wow!' gasped Pickle.

'Scrumpy, I did notice Oliver had some very strange-looking items around his neck and chest and on his golden belt, with bright, coloured buttons,' said Pal. 'And he had a golden star on his forehead.'

'A very interesting "teddy bear", hey Pal?' laughed Scrumpy, 'Patience! In time, you will all learn more about Oliver as you get to know him.'

'I just found him amazing! Wow!' uttered Pickle, who Pal knew had a tendency to hero-worship. Pal wondered, goodness knows what Pickle would be like when he actually met Oliver!

Patsy was daydreaming as she thought about all the colourful clothes worn by the inhabitants of Harmony Haven. She already had learnt from Scrumpy that all the moonling boys wore shirts and dungarees, and the girls, pretty dresses with striped stockings. This made her glow with happiness.

'Scrumpy, don't you think it's time we told the piglets about our two letters that Pickle saw me posting yesterday? Poor Pickle! He's been curious all day,' Pal said, panting.

Pickle oinked at his friend. 'I hope you're not implying that I'm a nosy piglet!

'Oh, just ignore him, Pickle!' squealed Patsy. 'He's only jealous that we can use our big snouts to have big kisses!' Patsy then started to rub her snout against Pickle's, which made him swoon with delight.

'Yuuuuck!' said Pal.

Scrumpy coughed, then looked serious. 'Do any of you want to hear what I have to say, or not?'

Pal, Pickle and Patsy all immediately stopped bickering and listened politely to Scrumpy.

'I will tell you what was in those letters, but before, I do I have some good news to impart, that I think you all should know,' he said, as the friends gathered around. 'Am I correct in thinking that many of your friends were going to Food Heaven this morning?'

The friends nodded, feeling sad and not knowing what to say.

'Despair not!' replied Scrumpy, his smile lightening

the mood. 'I can tell you that they have all been rescued, taken to a rescue centre and are safe and well!'

Scrumpy was delighted as he watched the three friends dancing together and shouting wildly with delight at the news. Until he asked, 'And shall I tell you about the letters that you were so desperate to learn about, Pickle?'

Pal wagged his tail. 'Oh, Scrumpy, please tell the piglets what we have been up to!' he sniggered.

Scrumpy grinned and began, 'I will, but I must tell you that what we did was rather mischievous, don't you think Pal?' said Scrumpy, winking at his doggy friend.

'No!' laughed Pal, 'It was jolly good fun!'

'What have you done? Played a joke, I suppose!' said Pickle, but he felt worried because he thought that Scrumpy may have led Pal into trouble.

Scrumpy continued, 'Well, the first letter we sent was very important. It was to the inspectors who checked that animals were being looked after. We told them that Farmer Muggleton had been ill-treating his animals and not giving them enough to eat. They would have got that letter today, you see.'

'That's great news, Scrumpy!' praised Pickle who could hardly believe what he was hearing.

Patsy was delighted as well, as she asked excitedly, 'And what about the second letter, Scrumpy? Because I'm nosy too, just like my husband! Oink! Oink!'

Her comments made them all grin at her.

'Perhaps you would like to explain about the second letter,' Scrumpy said, addressing Pal. 'Because *you* were involved as much as me.'

'Thanks, Scrumpy!' replied Pal. He looked at the piglets. 'Now, you won't know this, but if humans want to sell food to other humans, like "Muggleton's Sausages", the meat and food kitchens they use must be spotless and all the pots clean too!'

The two mischief makers began to laugh, so it was Scrumpy that continued with the story. 'So, our second letter went to the food inspectors, just letting them know that the Muggleton's food kitchens were filthy with ants and flies everywhere.'

'Goodness me!' gasped Pickle. 'I wish I had thought of doing what you two so cleverly had done!'

Pal continued to report on what they had done next. 'So, one night, when Scrumpy paid a visit to me, we collected cow dung, mouse droppings, a dead mouse, dead insects and rats, knowing these were going to be very handy.'

'Don't forget the flies, Pal!' added Scrumpy, as he screwed up his nose in disgust at what they had done, before continuing the story. 'And then, early this morning, I took everything into the meat kitchen. We knew the family would use their home kitchen and would be off in a hurry to get rid of the pigs, so they wouldn't see what Pal and I had done!'

'Crikey!' oinked Pickle, in praise of his friends. 'There is going to be some trouble when the inspectors call. That's great news! You both should be very proud of what you have done on behalf of all the farm animals at Muggleton's, because that was payback time!'

'Well done both of you. I'm very proud of you both,' said Patsy, who went to kiss Pal with her big snout, but Pal quickly pulled away and instead just barked happily at her.

'Scrumpy,' said Pickle, in an apologetic voice, 'I owe you a big apology. I thought you had led my friend astray, but it turns out that he is as bad as you with your playful nature!' He then turned to Patsy, 'Don't you think, my little piggy-wiggy, that we are so lucky to have these two as caring friends? Let's make a lot of noise to thank them for being two very special mischief makers!'

Scrumpy smiled at his friend and said, 'A job well done, Pal, don't you think?'

But Pal just grinned and watched the piglets showing that they were delighted in what the pair had done.

Scrumpy once again began to chuckle, knowing he had forgotten something. 'Oh, dear! I nearly forgot to tell you something, before we go on with the final part of our journey. I must mention—'

The three friends laughed as they shouted back at him. 'Never mention the word "MAGIC!" to Oliver Gruffle!'

Scrumpy nodded his head in agreement, as Pal, Pickle and Patsy laughed with him. But they were each thinking what a journey it had been so far, with so many new experiences and making new kindly friends. And how good it was to feel happy—yes, really happy!

But Pal was looking quizzically at his little moonling friend. 'We have had such wonderful adventures on our way here, Scrumpy. We have done things and seen things that none of us could ever imagine was possible. But, what I would really love to know is... will we have more exciting adventures on the last part of our journey?'

The little man smiled at the three happy-looking

friends that he had helped on their way to a better life. He gave one of his chuckles, smiled widely and said. 'Well, knowing Oliver Gruffle, like I do, I can tell you, your lives are going to be exciting and happy and there will be more exciting adventures to come! But please, remember, don't go saying the word "Magic" in front of Oliver, as I would hate to see you all get a long mouse's tail as punishment!'

The newcomers all laughed, and Scrumpy laughed too, wiping away tears of joy, while he looked at the three friends as they happily chatted about their new life and future adventures. Scrumpy also knew that, by helping others, no matter who or what they were, there was no better feeling than the feeling he was experiencing inside.

But, his thoughts were interrupted when Pal said, 'Come on, Scrumpy, lead the way! We are so looking forward to meeting Oliver Gruffle!'

Patsy and Pickle both oinked with joy at this.

Scrumpy clapped in joy. 'And do you know what your life is going to be like from now on...?'

Pal, Pickle and Patsy all smiled and yelled... in one loud voice... 'MAGICAL!'

THE END

Follow Pal, Pickle and Patsy's exciting adventures in BOOK 2! It'll be unbelievable and, of course... MAGICAL!

Lightning Source UK Ltd.
Milton Keynes UK
UKHW020844271120
374207UK00007B/419